# LEARNING TO DREAM

# LEARNING TO DREAM

## The New British Cinema

JAMES PARK

*faber and faber*

LONDON · BOSTON

First published in 1984
by Faber and Faber Limited
3 Queen Square London WC1N 3AU

Set by Goodfellow & Egan Ltd., Cambridge
Printed in Great Britain by
Redwood Burn & Co. Ltd., Trowbridge
All rights reserved

© James Park, 1984

*British Library Cataloguing in Publication Data*

Park, James
Learning to dream: the new British cinema.
1. Moving-picture industry – Great Britain
I. Title
384'.8'0941   PN1993.5.G7

ISBN 0-571-13401-7

# CONTENTS

ACKNOWLEDGEMENTS

---

This book could not have been written without the help of
Mundy Ellis, Mary-Jane Walsh, Nicholas Pole and Joyce
Corcos. Thanks also to all the film-makers who submitted to
interview: Andrew Birkin, Roger Christian, Al Clark, Bill
Douglas, Richard Eyre, Bill Forsyth, Stephen Frears, Brian
Gilbert, Peter Greenaway, Mamoun Hassan, Derek Jarman,
Roland Joffe, Neil Jordan, Marek Kanievska, Lynda Myles,
Pat O'Connor, Alan Parker, Chris Petit, David Puttnam,
Michael Radford, Nicolas Roeg, Peter Sainsbury, James
Scott, Julien Temple, Jeremy Thomas, Kenith Trodd.

# PART ONE

# CONTEXT

# 1

# EXCUSES

The history of British cinema has been one of unparalleled mediocrity. In the past, with the exception of a few major directors, British film-makers generally lacked the strength of vision necessary to explore cinema's potential to chart the furthest reaches of fantasy and extremes of passion. More recently, the containment of feeling that characterizes most television drama has been preferred to the soaring ambitions of cinema, the twentieth century's most potent medium. Words, and stories that can be neatly resolved, have had greater appeal than the adventurous poetry and ambiguity of images. Parochial television plays have been considered more significant than the cinema, a medium that can express its dramas across the barriers that divide classes and nations. To paraphrase a remark made by François Truffaut to Alfred Hitchcock, cinema and Britain have long seemed antithetical concepts.

In the early 1980s there was much talk about a new spirit in British cinema. *Chariots of Fire* and *Gandhi* carried off the Oscars successively in 1982 and 1983. *Gregory's Girl*, *Educating Rita* and *Experience Preferred – But Not Essential* attracted an enthusiastic response from American audiences, and in Europe critical plaudits were handed out to *The Draughtsman's Contract*, *Another Time, Another Place* and *Angel*. It seemed as if Britain's writers, directors and producers had finally found the inspiritation necessary to create a batch of films which could bear comparison with the output of any of the world's film industries. Yet some commentators considered these films only minor manifestations of cinematic competence. The director Alan Parker was not alone in characterizing the products of the 'new British cinema' as a 'plethora of narrow, often mediocre, work that has, in truth, had as much effect on the world's cinema as a plate of cold haggis'. Nicolas Roeg described the same films as 'nice movies lacking in originality, inventiveness, creativity, talent or art'.

In the enthusiastic search for a 'renaissance', many films of the period were overpraised, despite the fact that they made no advances in cinematic style or treatment of subject matter. Critics, excited at having something homegrown to write about, often failed to identify the defects of the British films. Film-makers, overjoyed that something was happening at last in British cinema, happily participated in the 'conspiracy of silence'. They were unable, or unwilling, to initiate any serious debate about how the British cinema could put aside the old myths and develop new aesthetic values. Mamoun Hassan, who for five years from 1979 attempted to initiate a revival of British feature production from his position as managing director of the National Film Finance Corporation (NFFC), expresses a widely felt feeling about the lack of intellectual weight brought by many of the new British film-makers to their task: 'We really do need to have a view of what it is that we are about. We seem totally uninterested in coming clean and joining with each other in a terrific battle as to what the films should be about.'

If many of the films made in the early 1980s had no claim to be part of any 'renaissance', the period was marked by a new ambition to create a British cinema, which will surely provide the basis for a unique and interesting period in the country's film history. A number of new directors have emerged from various training grounds, equipped with an understanding of film and a desire to tackle the problems involved in creating a British cinema. Those directors who graduated from the National Film School (NFS), founded in

1971, had a grasp of film technique and a knowledge of the history of world cinema acquired from the school's three-year training programme. Their films represented a diverse set of concerns, reflecting their personal proclivities for different subject matter and cinematic traditions. While Michael Radford finds his roots in the work of the French *nouvelle vague* and Italian cinema, Roger Christian combines a personal sympathy for the work of Ingmar Bergman, Roman Polanski and Akira Kurosawa, with an insider's knowledge of the workings of Hollywood's dream factory. Julien Temple expresses a keen interest in the forms of American popular cinema, but his own work is motivated by an interest in British history and the roots of contemporary youth culture, while Brian Gilbert, the most recent graduate from the school in this group, looks to the aesthetics of Jean Renoir and François Truffaut for his forays into the codes and attitudes of middle-class society. Bill Forsyth, who stayed only a short time at the school but remained within its cultural orbit, applies a similar perspective to Gilbert's, on his lower middle-class Scottish world.

Equally varied approaches to film are adopted by those who come to film-directing along other routes. The British Film Institute Production Board provided both Chris Petit, whose concerns as film critic and film-maker were with contemporary European cinema, and Peter Greenaway, who lists in his cultural baggage both the aesthetics of land art and the intellectual games of the post-modernist movement, with the opportunity to channel their personal aesthetic concerns into an accessible form of cinema. Roland Joffe and Marek Kanievska both emerged from the restrictions of television to seek out cinema's larger canvas as a medium to explore political concerns, while the preoccupations of the senior Stephen Frears were tied up in questions of style and personal expression. These directors, together with Irish novelist Neil Jordan, Irish documentarist Pat O'Connor, screenwriter Andrew Birkin, artist Derek Jarman, and James

Scott, who emerged from low-budget film-making, form an informal group with sufficient grasp of the potential of the film medium to create a cinema that is both acutely personal and yet capable of reaching large audiences worldwide.

As long as the finance can be found for these film-makers to develop their art, they will provide the backbone for the development of a new British cinema that is broader and more diverse than anything previously produced in Britain. While recognizing that skilled writers, producers and cameramen are also essential to the development of a new British cinema, this book attempts to explore the roots of current developments by articulating the views of these particular film-makers. The director is the linchpin of the production process. Without directorial excellence, creative brilliance in other areas can make no impact.

It should occasion no surprise that these directors do not constitute an easily defined movement. They share no common set of references to trends in contemporary art or literature. They have not felt, like the Free Cinema movement of the late 1950s, the need to define their position against a 'snobbish, anti-intellectual and second-rate' film-industry establishment. Their opportunity to make films has been created on a *tabula rasa*, where newly developed sources of finance are looking to back not the feeble remnants of an old British cinema, but anyone who seems capable of taking British films to new heights of commercial success and critical acclaim. In attempting to find a form to express their personal concerns, these directors draw not only on the traditions of world cinema, but also on other artistic and literary influences to which they have been exposed. In time the doors of opportunity may start to close, but for the moment the one factor uniting both the new film-makers and the financiers is a search for new ways to realize the potential of cinema and to rise above the limitations of television. It is for the diversity of cinema, not its orthodoxy, for a variety of approaches to subject matter, for the generation of new forms and the intelligent discarding of the superannuated, that the new British film-makers must campaign.

The television medium provides the main touchstone for the current debate not only because of its dominant role as the producer of audiovisual forms, but also because its limitations reflect upon the failures of British cinema and culture in the past. In fighting television the new British film-makers are attempting to do more than make films that apply realist modes to contemporary subject matter, or retreat into nostalgic anachronisms. They are attempting to create a space in which to explore the range of human emotions through forms that are innovative, stylish and visually exciting. They are demanding the right to be passionate, subversive and intellectually profound. Their strength comes from a new awareness of the many bridges that have to be crossed in order to form a vital British film culture.

Until now the ardour with which the practitioners of television have defended the medium, accusing those who campaigned for a cinema industry of snobbishness and élitism, has frustrated any significant discussion about the limitations of a televisual aesthetic. While television has provided scope for the stylistic talents of film-makers such as Ken Loach and Stephen Frears and occasionally allowed relatively personal concerns to be explored in film, the predominant preoccupation of the best television film drama has been with the exploration of contemporary political and social concerns, rather than the full use of the film medium. Television's high points are represented in works of documentary-style realism, from Ken Loach's *Cathy Come Home* to Alan Clarke's *Made in Britain* which, while technically proficient and cast in a form that is adequate for their subject matter, lack both the universality and the ambitions of a cinema film. As Alan Parker says of the latter work: 'It is articulate, absolutely relevant to our culture, society, political problems and every aspect of our life. It is wonderful that we do it, but I don't think for one moment that it is anything to do with cinema.' Even many of the supposedly

17

cinematic works financed by Channel Four Television have been cast in the same mould.

British television began to change in the early 1980s. As its executives responded to the initial impact of video, they also grasped that the fragmentation of the market which would follow the arrival of new forms of image distribution, such as cable and satellite, would entail a prolonged struggle to hold on to audiences. The consequent developments only lessened the value of television for creative film-makers. The BBC became less interested in finding new ways to explore contemporary subjects in drama than in padding out its ratings with imported American series and making costume drama for the international market with all the compromises that this entailed. The shrinking finances of the commercial television companies caused resources to be concentrated on blockbuster series such as *Reilly, Ace of Spies, The Jewel in the Crown, Kennedy* and popular video productions, rather than providing a space for gutsy and entertaining films. Only Central Television, which financed *Made in Britain* as part of a series of four films written by David Leland and Stephen Frears' *The Hit*, seemed willing to resist the new financial pressures.

These developments only highlighted the problems involved in working within British television. Realism is the most appropriate form for the television dramatist wishing to explore the moral codes and social values of contemporary society. The appearance of documentary objectivity renders politically committed drama acceptable to an institution that is established and monitored by governments and must adhere to certain principles relating to political balance and aesthetic taste. Films that employed more subjective and imaginative approaches would automatically be regarded with suspicion by a mentality that is more concerned with journalism than free creation. The supposed liberalization of the medium through the new media will necessarily bring in its wake commercial pressures that will drive television films towards the escapism of boulevard theatre rather than challenging new heights. The international co-productions on which the television companies are now concentrating their finances have no relevance to contemporary British society and attitudes and in seeking to appeal to a mass audience in a relatively undemanding way, reflect no interest in any value other than simple-minded entertainment.

The failure of the British television companies before the arrival of Channel Four to imitate their European counterparts and provide finance for film-making outside the constraints of television's own bureaucratic structures has left British film-makers with only one option – the making of films that depict the day-to-day realities of life. By contrast, f¹m-makers in German;, Italy and France have been able to use the resources of television that explore the devices of cinema to stir the emotions of participants and encourage them to question both the nature of their lives and the values of the society in which they are placed. 'In the end,' suggests Chris Petit, 'everything in England goes back to the concept of the establishment and the anti-establishment. One of the greatest strengths of the English establishment is that it has always incorporated the anti-establishment, which is why there have been very few iconoclastic directors in this country.'

Behind the restrictions imposed upon television film-makers by the institution, and the fact that their work is destined to be received on a small screen that domesticates even the strongest human emotions, lies a peculiarly British suspicion of passion and emotional commitment. The stiff-upper-lip mentality has been evident throughout the history of British cinema, which has generally failed to expose the complexity of human life and the fullness of people's longings for a different world. England may once have produced William Shakespeare, but Michael Radford recalls seeing a BBC production of *Measure for Measure*: 'You were being told about the passions that the people in the play had for each other, but you weren't feeling them and being engaged in them. You were merely meant to stand back and watch.

19

But the great films engage you passionately, they make you laugh, they make you cry, they make you angry, they make you feel things.' For a television film-maker like Ken Loach, the capacity of cinema to manipulate and stir its audience is a taint that stands in the way of an objective appreciation of human reality, but cinema is a subjective medium which rises to greatness only when the emotions conveyed are deeply felt and skilfully stirred. 'The British,' Roger Christian remarks, 'tend to sit back and be very undemonstrative and unemotional. I think it is a good time to get emotional. That is what breeds good literature and great art. I wish that the film-makers here would be more brave.'

Another problem which manifests itself particularly in television is the strength of anti-intellectual currents in British culture, which seem to spring from middle-class guilt about its own sophistication. Cinema aspires to reach a large audience, not an élite, but too often in British film history, populism and commercial ambition have been confused with mediocrity. Within television the rule has been that new subjects should be explored in accepted ways, but it is only through experiments with style and form and a willingness to reject the received ideas about how films should be made, that films can emerge which will truly excite an audience. Many who have set themselves up as film producers in Britain are as suspicious of cinematic adventure as their counterparts in television and base their judgements on a distrust of culture, conceived as élitism, which is a peculiarly British syndrome. 'There is a swamping middlebrow quality,' suggests Michael Radford, 'to most British culture. It's the kind of Hampstead, BBC2, *Sunday Times* colour supplement axis. We are very good at producing a middlebrow analysis of things, but not fantastically good at producing something of really high aesthetic quality, or works that are gripping and popular.' More laconically Peter Greenaway observes: 'I am interested in a cinema of ideas, which is basically not the British predicament.'

Throughout the 1960s and 1970s the battle against these

anti-intellectual attitudes was fought largely in the ghetto of experimental film-making. Politically committed film-makers and those concerned to explore the aesthetics of film, repudiated the traditions of cinema and the forms of television. The manipulative qualities of cinema and its use of visual trickery came under attack and was analysed as the 'pleasure principle'. Subversive political messages were hammered home with a sledge-hammer rather than subtly explored within a narrative framework. The very use of narrative was condemned as expression of a tacit acceptance of bourgeois realities. The use of star performers and the visual gloss of high-budget film-making and anything that would make films accessible to audiences was treated with suspicion. A sophisticated range of intellectual theories expressed through a web of obscurantism were articulated to explain and justify this approach to cinema. Films such as *Riddles of the Sphinx* and *The Song of the Shirt* represented the primal scream of those alienated from contemporary currents in British culture and society.

Television's concern with good writing and political commitment in preference to visual style and cinematic ambitions also derives from a culture that places little emphasis on the visual arts and gives little guidance to the young in how to appreciate cinema. The fault is perpetuated by many of those who criticize or write about film and manifest in their work a deep lack of awareness about the achievements of world cinema and a profound level of cinematic illiteracy. Any form of innovation, any attempt to create striking imagery that may move audiences in new ways, is dismissed as pretension. What is worrying about such writing is the absence of any serious attempt to convey to the reader what a particular film-maker has sought to achieve. For example, Nicolas Roeg's innovative and passionate *Bad Timing* used a complex series of flashbacks to explore the search for emotional and sexual fulfilment within a relationship betweeen an American psychoanalyst and a passionate but flighty English girl. One reviewer

21

dismissed the film's technique as a 'plethora of camera side-swipes at chi-chi cultural items, fed as false fodder to those who rejoice in making pseudo-intellectual connections of no relevance to anything'. What particularly gave him the 'trots' was the 'overall style which plays merry hell with chronology'. The review ended with a gratuitous attempt at wit: 'I can't resist adding that *Bad Timing* sometimes looks like the longest cigarette commercial ever, in the most literal sense a drag from beginning to end.' If such a critical method was applied to art, literature or music, its lack of sophistication would be clearly revealed.

While many critics for the 'quality' papers do go about their task with greater seriousness, the lack of intelligent film criticism is demoralizing for British film-makers. Directors need critics not only to help an audience to understand and take an interest in their work, but also to assure them that someone is making an effort to comprehend the deeper levels in their films. Bill Forsyth compares the English critics unfavourably to both their European and American counterparts: 'No matter that film-makers are attempting some kind of personal film-making, the critics don't seem capable of making that same journey. If anything is going to happen to film culture in this country, it requires something more from the critics. I would respect any opinion of my work if I could see the logic of it.' Stephen Frears observes that most film-makers develop the style of their films in a relatively instinctive way and need critical feedback: 'I'm trying to find people who will discuss what one is doing seriously. I've never met anyone in England who could say why a shot had the elements in it that I've put into it, why it was lit the way it was, what weight it had, how the movements in it worked.'

Where the critical tradition is not both anti-intellectual and anti-art, the books and articles that have been written have done little towards establishing a set of criteria for the formation of a British film culture. Serious attempts to examine the relevance of the past and present achievements in British cinema for a new generation of film-makers are rare. Indeed, the work of Britain's major film directors has generally been decried. Alfred Hitchcock made the grade by emigrating to America, but there has been little examination of the works of Robert Hamer and Alexander Mackendrick which, within the generally frivolous context of Ealing Studios, did explore the darker sides of human nature. Only one serious book has been written on the passionate and subversive output of Hammer Studios, while the work of Michael Powell, Carol Reed and David Lean has been largely neglected. More recently the baroque brilliance of Ken Russell (*Women in Love, The Devils, Altered States*) has been dismissed as indulgent; the depth of human emotions explored in the work of Nicolas Roeg (*Walkabout, Don't Look Now, Eureka*) and the potency of his experimentation with the film medium, have been felt as mere incoherence. 'We have really painted ourselves into a corner,' suggests Mamoun Hassan. 'When the critics and intellectuals attack every aspect of British film-making, then they cannot be surprised that we are all without roots. Those people who have been able to see that quite a lot of the criticism is half-baked and ignorant have survived, but the responsibility of the critics is quite considerable.'

In the absence of a British cinema with any sense of direction, British film-makers have felt the weight of other film cultures as a heavy burden. The most active international film industry is, of course, that of Hollywood. For many British film-makers Los Angeles has been the mecca, providing them with funds for major productions and a stimulating approach to the craft of film largely lacking in the British scene. For as long as the British have made films UK financiers have pursued international success by imitating the form of American films, rather than searching for British modes to explore native subjects. Many of the new directors find their inspiration in European cinema as they attempt to develop new approaches to British film. Michael Radford keeps a room in Paris where he goes to write: 'Despite the fact that French cinema is going through a terrible crisis at the moment, the French care about film practically more than anyone else. Ordinary people will be very knowledgeable and have ideas and give you feedback.' For Derek Jarman, the frame of reference is Italy: 'The cinema is recognized as an art form in Italy, and they have this attitude to their cinema which makes it one of the really wonderful and fascinating cinemas. There is nothing like that here.'

Radford describes the sense of inferiority generated by the smallness of Britain's cinematic heritage as a stimulus to creative activity: 'I think there's something in the shame that we feel here which is stimulating Britain more than anywhere else at the moment. There is a real sense that British film culture should mean something.' The early 1980s did in fact provide a relatively clear field in which British filmmakers could make an impression, and the general crisis in world cinema partly explains the enthusiasm with which British films were greeted in many of the world's markets. In America the cost accountants and market analysts had taken over the studios and spent their millions on a string of teen pictures pandering to the basest aspirations of America's youth, and on gargantuan science fiction epics that concealed their lack of content behind a panoply of special effects. The great Italian-American stylists, Francis Ford Coppola and Martin Scorsese, found it increasingly difficult to find new subjects that would trigger their poetic vision of American life. In Europe the transformation of the media, with the concept of television broadening to include cable, satellite and various other ways of transferring images to the small screen, has caused a sense of uncertainty among filmmakers. This was reflected in the uneven output of many European directors. The only fresh voices were those of the Third World, from Latin America to Africa and the Far East.

Those who campaigned during the 1970s for a revival of the British film industry made little attempt to analyse the deficiencies of British film culture. Their preoccupation was to impress upon a largely disinterested government the need for state intervention to stimulate production. This case was put most clearly by the Association of Independent Producers (AIP), formed in 1976, which argued that the dominance of American productions in the market-place worked against the emergence of indigenous films. If the government, it argued, developed a system of subsidy for the British production, distribution and exhibition sectors, modelled on the aid schemes established in France and Germany, then British cinema would be able to take its place alongside the great cinemas of the world. The AIP called for more funds to be channelled to the National Film Finance Corporation, to enable it to assist the commercial industry in the financing of medium-budget (£1 million – £2 million) film production projects. The television companies were exhorted to recognize that their schedules depended on a steady supply of feature films, and to make production finance available to British film producers. The Monopolies Commission was approached with proposals for the breaking up of the two major cinema circuits which exercised a stranglehold over the exhibition sector. The Department of Trade was called upon to establish a sales organization to market British films internationally.

The AIP's campaign was largely a failure. Government indifference ensured that none of its central policy aims could be achieved. At the beginning of 1984 the NFFC's continued existence was in question; major television network companies were doing little to stimulate feature film production; Rank and Thorn EMI remained firmly in control of their cinemas; and no film marketing authority had been established. The AIP might claim that the interest which it had stirred in the possibility of creating a British cinema had borne fruit in the early 1980s but in fact the Association had never clearly articulated the case for cinema. It did not attempt to answer the question, 'what films?' beyond a loosely phrased call for 'indigenous' movies springing from British life and attitudes which would provide an alternative to the 'international pap' emanating from various British-based companies. Other forces lay behind the revival of British film-making activity.

The new sources of finance for film production that emerged in the early 1980s were stimulated not only by the arrival at their creative maturity of a bevy of film-makers keen to break through the pattern of mediocrity that has characterized so much of British cinema history, but also by various structural changes in the industry. Channel Four's film policy meant that television could now be looked upon as a partner in the production of low-budget feature films, rather than an institution that secured the largest audience for films which it had purchased at minimal cost. The developments in the video market and the prospect of an expanding market for films, thanks to the arrival of cable and satellite television internationally, all created a flurry of interest in the financing of audiovisual 'software'. This has created an environment which, for the moment at least, is sympathetic to new ideas and forms. While the new companies have often financed work that is mediocre, and made choices that were felt to be 'safe', they have also encouraged a new confidence amongst British film-makers. David Puttnam points out that 'if you are confident when going into a project, that you are going to make a picture, you can then start addressing the material in your own terms'. With that sense of conviction you can impress upon the sources of finance the 'need to seek out new subjects and explore them in new ways'.

What produced these new film-makers, seemingly characterized by a strength of vision that enabled them to transcend the limitations of previous British cinema? Many of the new directors of the early 1980s had spent their formative years in the early 1960s. They inherited from that period the concern for individual self-expression and opposition to the stultifying effects of British institutions and traditional attitudes. The Free Cinema film-makers of the early 1960s expressed many of the concerns of the period – sexual liberation, an opening-up of Britain's repressive class structure and a transformation in the educational system. Today's film-makers were forming their attitudes to life in response to the same winds of change. Peter Greenaway and Derek Jarman were at art school. Julien Temple was listening to rock music when the lights were down in his boarding school dormitory, and Roland Joffe was skiving off school games to catch such films as *Darling* and *Saturday Night and Sunday Morning*. James Scott made his first film in 1962 but found the Free Cinema film-makers' preoccupation with working-class issues restricting and alien to his more personal concerns.

For the directors who made films in the 1960s the dashing of the hopes expressed in that period encourages cynicism and despair about cinema today. Lindsay Anderson concludes from the state of contemporary Britain that a vigorous film culture is impossible: 'The cinema gives a clear indication of the nation's morale, vitality, creativity. The cinema can reflect, can stimulate the vitality of a nation, but it cannot *create* that vitality.' The symbol of the 1980s for Nicolas Roeg is the forlorn and bedraggled demeanour of the post-punk Mohican, 'ready for the Gulag'. He suggests that, with the social and political retrenchment of the 1980s, 'it is not a creative time for the arts'.

For the new British film-makers the dreams of the 1960s, matured by subsequent history, influence their attitude to the shoddiness of the modern world. The escapist currents in contemporary youth culture and the output of television drive them to grapple with the only audiovisual medium that can approach the deeper problems affecting individual psyches and the national mood. For many the policies pursued by Margaret Thatcher and Ronald Reagan, with their concern for the material aspects of human life – economic growth, efficiency, productivity – stand in stark opposition to the preoccupation of cinema to give some sense of the meaning of life and to direct audiences to the potential of their existence. The films of the new directors do not reflect the slick vacuity of such contemporary rock bands as Spandau

Ballet, Duran Duran or ABC, nor current 1960s nostalgia. Their roots are in the best of rock 'n' roll, with its passionate project to liberate the individual from the shackles of English society. Films such as Marek Kanievska's *Another Country*, Michael Radford's *1984*, Roland Joffe's *The Killing Fields* and Pat O'Connor's *Cal* all contribute to the debate about the future of Britain and the world.

To make films which do more than tell a good story or give a respectable account of day-to-day life requires considerable imagination and the courage to confront issues. In the late 1960s and the 1970s, when political issues were explored outside television, the approach adopted was often a simplistic recourse to heavy-handed agitprop or marginalized experimentation. Film-makers who developed more personal concerns generally lacked the depth of inner conviction necessary to penetrate beneath the surface. Many of the new film-makers, by contrast, have a grasp of the possibilities of cinematic style, a desire for personal expression that cannot be satisfied with merely realizing a script idea fed through a factory process, and an aspiration to communicate their feelings to a large audience which is strong enough to drive them away from vapid commercialism, private film-making and ghetto art. Only history can judge how successful the new British film-makers will be in creating a body of work that means something in the context of world cinema, but the aspiration to work in that direction is in itself a fresh and encouraging development.

It is the dreams of these directors and the producers who have supported their efforts which are explored in this book. The first part examines the backgrounds of the various directors and the transformations in the industry which have facilitated their film-making efforts. Subsequent pages look in detail at their creative ambitions, outlining the way in which these film-makers define cinema and their distinctive approach to subjects and cinematic style.

# 2

# ROUTES

The route that a director takes towards his or her feature must allow both for the development of a personal vision and the acquisition of an understanding of the potential of the film medium. When film-making was a continuous activity carried out in a studio context it was possible for an apprentice director to attach himself to a variety of feature projects and participate in the processes of film production before graduating to the position of a director. This was a potentially stimulating process that exposed the novice to the values of feature films, though giving little opportunity for the development of an individual voice. With the arrival of television in the late 1950s came more erratic patterns of film production and the effective closing down of the apprenticeship route, although directors have occasionally emerged from other technical departments. In many European countries and in America the film industry responded by setting up film academies to provide basic training, a course adopted in Britain with the establishment of the National Film School in 1970. However, television itself provided other ways into feature film-making. In the 1960s John Boorman, John Schlesinger and Ken Russell developed their knowledge of the medium within the BBC, firstly making personal documentaries, then more ambitious drama projects. The most successful directors of the 1970s, such as Alan Parker and Ridley Scott, learnt their craft through the manufacture of numerous television commercials. More

29

recently the development of video and cable television has encouraged record companies, hit by declining sales, to produce video clips to promote new singles, and this has opened up another training area for young hopefuls.

All these training grounds provide young directors with an approximation to the world of feature film-making, and each emphasizes different aspects of the abilities required of a director. In commercials the emphasis is on style rather than content. Television drama, by contrast, offers an opportunity to explore personal subject matter without providing the resources necessary for a full use of the potential of the film medium. In pop promos the director can develop his own scripts and use film in a creative way, but the fact that the image must always take second place to the music means that work in this form is often very undisciplined. Film schools provide an opportunity for students to acquire a personal style and develop an appreciation of subject matter without exposing them to the rigours of commercial film-making. Although seminars are regularly organized around the theme of how best to educate a film director, the truth is that anyone with the ambition to make feature films must seize any opportunity offered to him, but always remain conscious of the deficiencies inherent in his training ground. Increasingly, graduates from the NFS have recognized that fact by following up their school training with work in commercials, pop promos and other forms of pre-feature film-making, in the belief that through a broader experience of the possibilities of the medium in all its forms, they will find it easier to develop a style corresponding to their own imagination.

In fact, most of the directors who come to features through commercials have a more diverse experience of film-making than they are given credit for. Tony Scott, director of *The Hunger,* trained at the Royal College of Art, and made two short films, *One of the Missing* and *Loving Memory,* before starting to work in commercials. Terry Bedford, who made the thriller *Slayground,* studied at the

London International Film School then worked as a camera-man for Ridley Scott, Adrian Lyne and Hugh Hudson before starting to direct commercials in his own right. He also made the television play *Freedom of the Dig* for the BBC. Richard Loncraine combined work on commercials with directing such television dramas as Granada's *The Secret Orchards* and LWT's *Blade on the Feather*, before becoming a fully fledged feature director with *Brimstone and Treacle* and *The Missionary*. Graduates from the NFS who have been signed up by commercials companies include Stephen Bayly, Terry Winsor and Brian Gilbert. 'It is an opportunity', says Gilbert, 'to keep working, thinking dramatically and expressively in film. You get a better understanding of the technical qualities and continuously stretch yourself.'

For those who work too long in commercials and are perhaps lacking a strong personal vision, the experience can mar their work with an excessive reliance on stylistic effects. Newspaper critics are quick to apply the label 'vacuous' to the work of commercials-trained directors. David Robinson, writing in *The Times,* once described 'working in television commercials as a taint rather than a training, with the handicaps of having learnt to work in isolated couplets rather than poetry; in show-off arpeggios and fancy trills rather than musical compositions'. The charge is not without weight, and it is up to each commercials director to find a way to compensate for his training, especially as many American studios will encourage novice graduates from the commercials school to apply maximum gloss to any films that they make.

This was a problem confronted by Roger Christian, who worked as a set decorator (*Star Wars*) and art director (*Alien, Life of Brian*) before enrolling at the National Film School to prepare for a career as a film director: 'I like narrative films, but having come from the art department, everyone thinks that I'm going to make visual but empty films.' At the school Christian self-consciously concentrated on learning to write and understand literary values. His

31

short film, *The Dollar Bottom,* which won him an Academy Award, depended largely on the text and performances for its impact. And although his first feature *The Sender,* about a boy with the capacity to project his thoughts and dreams into the consciousness of others, could easily have become a special effects display, Christian deliberately gave the film a documentary look. The financiers responded negatively to this restrained shooting style. *The Sender* was given only a limited release in the USA and was not distributed internationally.

Commercials allow directors the time and resources to experiment freely with the medium. Hugh Hudson, the director of *Chariots of Fire* and *Greystoke,* once compared the process of having to produce only thirty seconds a day of usable footage (as opposed to two or four minutes on a medium-budget feature production) to the perfectionism applied in the making of Swiss watches. 'In some ways,' says Terry Bedford, 'it is the best shooting experience you can get, because the pressure isn't so intense, and you can treat it more like you're enjoying yourself.' It can also be a good opportunity to develop relationships with cameramen, art directors and editors, which provide valuable learning experience for the director and serve as the basis for future creative partnerships.

However, the lifestyle and the luxury of relaxed schedules and inflated budgets can create problems for commercials directors when they attempt to break into features. Film-making is, by comparison with commercials, not a lucrative profession. Few commercials-trained directors have tried their hand at low- or medium-budget film-making where development of narrative is more important than stylistic fireworks. Commercials directors tend to gravitate towards Hollywood where they can apply their visual virtuosity to a high-budget chintzy work rather than chance their arm on a gritty piece of contemporary drama. The reliance on technique is magnified as commercials directors work on ready-made scripts provided by an advertising agency and rarely have an opportunity to write or develop their own scripts.

Furthermore, the commercials director is everyday soaking up a view of the world that is antithetical to the mission of the artist to examine and question the world around him. 'Obviously,' says Brian Gilbert, 'if you are working in commercials, they may have a terribly detrimental effect on you, because you learn to work to certain briefs that affect you. Most people who are directors are perfectionists and want to do it as well as they can, meeting the standards of competence that are required. Technically the standards of competence required by commercials may be terrific, but you are still selling Persil and it's not the same as realizing a piece of drama.'

The production of visual accompaniments to popular songs, based either on a live performance or a concept inspired by the music, is as old as the technology synchronizing sound and image, but it was only with the development in the early 1980s of America's twenty-four-hour Music Television (MTV) cable channel that it became common practice for record companies to commission pop promos as marketing tools for new singles. These short items are designed to generate an awareness of a piece of music through screenings on the music cable services, network television's pop programmes, and also as videos sold through retail outlets. The popularity of British bands in America during the early 1980s is often attributed to the stylishness of the associated promos screened on MTV and in consequence business has boomed in Britain for the numerous British promo production companies. A few directors, notably Steve Barron and Russell Mulcahy, have already moved from promos to their first features.

Superficially the pop promo offers a training ground with many similarities to commercials. The director is again learning how to sell an image, which relates to a particular group's view of itself. The style of the promo must be slick and instantly accessible if it is to convey its message in the limited time available. However, pop promo directors, unlike their counterparts working in commercials, do have the opportunity to develop their own scripts, albeit in close co-operation with the group whose music they are illustrating, and to develop a set of personal concerns around the ideas expressed in that music.

The fact that the budgets for pop promos are generally much tighter than for commercials imposes a set of disciplines on the director that are similar to those that apply in medium- and low-budget film-making. 'Pop promos,' observes Julien Temple, who has made many promos since leaving the National Film School, 'teach you to shoot very fast and force you to organize your thoughts very clearly and quickly.'

At their worst pop promos are undisciplined and banal. As they do not have to tell a story, visual ideas are often strung together with little regard for meaning or impact. The use of video allows the director to shoot endless undisciplined footage while video special effects provide a bizarre repertoire of devices with which to conceal the lack of a controlling concept. However, the director who understands the values required to communicate meaning to an audience, can use the opportunity offered by making promos to explore the medium in imaginative ways and make powerful, if compressed, statements. Julien Temple, who directed *The Great Rock 'n' Roll Swindle* before making his first promos, points out that the quality of a pop promo often depends upon the sophistication of the music around which the images are created. He himself prefers to work with mature bands like The Rolling Stones and The Kinks, rather than with what he describes as the 'teddy bear Kleenex groups', whose superficial view of the world is matched in the images 'inspired' by their performances. His Stones video, *Undercover*, was an attempt to question the way in which the media represents violence in El Salvador and other world trouble-spots, and much of Temple's work expresses his concern, otherwise explored in his films and television documentaries, with what it means to be young and English in Thatcher's Britain.

34

Steve Barron's promo work shows the extent to which a director with an awareness of film and an ambition to explore the medium can develop a personal vision through promo work. He makes all his promos in the form of 'mini-features', casting each one in a quasi-narrative structure and experimenting with different cinematic styles and genres. A consistent set of visual concerns emerge in his work with groups that include OMD, Japan and Heaven 17, character-ized by his use of stark studio sets, an expressive moving camera and an interest in the way in which people look at each other. In 1983 Barron attempted to develop these concerns in a film, *Electric Dreams*. Temple also tries to capture the aesthetics of cinema in his pieces, while knowing that most promos will only be seen on the small screen: 'The main pay-off for me is when I see the print in the viewing theatre.' Other directors who have done interesting work in pop promos include Derek Jarman, the director of *Sebastiane, Jubilee* and *The Tempest*; Ian Emes, an animator and director of two short films, *The Magic Shop* and *Goody Two Shoes*; Charles Sturridge, who made *Brideshead Revisited* and *Runners*; and former 10CC group members, Kevin Godley and Lol Creme, who will make *Hooverville* in 1985.

Television drama provides a training group that is in many ways the antithesis to commercials and pop promos. Those who work on studio video productions have to realize a narrative script and convey subject matter, rather than appeal to emotional responses through visual style. The same applies, to a lesser degree, for those who work in film. For the director who aspires to cinema it can be a very narrowing discipline. 'If you go into television,' said Sandy Lieberson, head of product-ion at Goldcrest Films since the beginning of 1984, 'you are totally orientated to producing films for television, and you have to put aside the interest in cinema and get on with making television programmes. It is very difficult to break out of it, because television can channel your sights and sensitivities in a certain way.'

Although various directors have used the opportunities

provided by working on film for television to develop a personal style, there is no forum within the television companies for the development of film aesthetics. One of television's most distinguished stylists is Stephen Frears, who moved out of the theatre initially to work as an assistant director, and then moved on to make films on his own. His first production, *The Burning*, was a short piece about an uprising in South Africa as seen by an old woman and her son, which revealed Frears's instinctive understanding of how to use the space available within the cinema screen for emotional effect. However, Frears himself emphasizes that it was only through making a large number of television films and working with a range of cinematographers, that he discovered the range of expression possible with a moving camera. A turning point was the making of *Going Gently*, a film for the BBC about two men dying of cancer. Smooth floor surfaces allowed for a freedom of camera movement not otherwise possible on location, and the nature of the subject called for poetic treatment. Frears has since developed his use of the camera in the melodrama *Loving Walter, Saigon* and *The Hit*, but he questions the significance of his concern with visual style in the context of television drama: 'People really like those domestic dramas, and if you make something that involves something larger than that, in terms of movement and light, maybe it's silly making them for television. Maybe one should just flog away on the end of the lens.'

What characterizes all the directors who make the transition from television to features is a consciousness of the larger ambition required for a cinema film and the need for a distinct stylistic input from the director. Michael Newell, director of *Dance for a Stranger*, said of his previous feature film *Bad Blood*, which was financed by television but distributed as a feature outside Brtitain: 'In my own mind, I was always making a feature. I think you have to approach it that way round. If it's a good film it will work on television. If I had said to myself, "I am making a television movie which can be shown in the cinemas too," that would have been death.'

Marek Kanievska, who graduated through *Coronation Street* and the *Muck and Brass* television series about municipal corruption in the Midlands to the feature film, *Another Country*, emphasizes: 'Although I'm from a traditional background that doesn't mean that with certain ideas and certain projects one wouldn't like to stand on its head what people expect to find on the screen, and turn the whole thing completely upside down.' Other directors who have crossed the divide include Michael Apted, director of *The Coalminer's Daughter* and *Gorky Park*; Ferdinand Fairfax, who followed his television series *Winston Churchill: The Wilderness Years* with *Savage Islands*, an adventure story set in New Zealand; Franc Roddam, the maker of *Quadrophenia* and *The Lords of Discipline*; and Gavin Millar, the director of *Secrets* and the fantasy feature *Dreamchild*.

Several of the directors who have come out of television originally worked in the theatre. 'I had always wanted to make films,' says Richard Eyre, 'but I got sidetracked into the theatre, and there was always something coming up that was too good to resist.' Eyre joined the BBC as a producer in 1978, and subsequently worked as a television director before breaking into features with *The Ploughman's Lunch*, *Loose Connections* and *Laughterhouse*. Roland Joffe, the director of *The Killing Fields*, is described by the film's producer, David Puttnam, as 'someone who just kept on the move and, every time something became a drag, he moved on'. Like Eyre, Joffe testifies to an early fascination with movies, but he left university with the intention of becoming either a painter or a sculptor. He became involved in theatre firstly through running a young people's group in Leicester, then in the setting-up of the Young Vic, which he welcomed as an opportunity to learn about working with actors. A training scheme run by Granada Television, which involved him in a range of programmes from current affairs to *Coronation Street*, taught him 'a kind of nerve and an ability to think under pressure'. He moved into heavyweight drama with *Bill Brand*, a series about a Labour politician written by Trevor Griffiths, then developed such highly charged and politically committed television dramas as *Legion Hall Bombing, Spongers* and *United Kingdom*, before being commissioned by Puttnam to make his first feature, an account of the bloodbath that followed the fall of Cambodia in 1975.

Opportunities to make film drama within television are increasingly limited. Neither the BBC nor the main ITV network companies provide many openings for those who have acquired their mastery of film outside television, particularly at the National Film School, to work on television films. For many, television documentary provides not only an easier route into the television companies, but a better way to explore the potential of the film medium than drama. Whereas the television dramatist has to work from a script commissioned by the producer, the documentary director has the freedom to formulate his own approach to a subject. The documentaries made by all those who have later graduated to features do not reflect television's persistent concern with the journalistic values of detachment and balance, but are subjective accounts of people and groups. Documentaries offer the film-maker an opportunity to explore the relations between style and subject, and to develop his knowledge of the world to a degree not possible for any of his counterparts in other training grounds.

Michael Radford, a graduate from the National Film School who spent eight years working on television documentaries, points out that, because of the strength of the British documentary tradition, the philosophical debate about documentary is far in advance of discussions about drama film-making. He considers such work as Michael Grigsby's film on the Inuit, Chris Menges's account of *East 103rd Street*, and Jana Bokova's *Sunset People*, to be more sophisticated in their use of the film medium than many films made for television or cinema. The documentary area provides an easier platform for debates about style and treatment of subject matter because the subject is autonomous and exists whether it is filmed or not, whereas the debate about drama is often limited to the question of what subject should be filmed. Radford's only television film *The White Bird Passes*, and first feature, *Another Time, Another Place*, both share stylistic concerns developed in his documentary work. The feature film explores the moral dilemma that confronts a young Scottish wife who starts to question the values of the dour Scottish community in which she lives, when a passionate Neapolitan is lodged on her farm as a POW. Its approach has its roots in two of Radford's documentaries: *The Last Stronghold of the Pure Gospel*, which illuminated Protestantism in a northern community by showing the climate and countryside, and through a very formal relationship between camera and subject; and *The Madonna and the Volcano*, which used a more fluid camera style to explore the traditions of Neapolitan catholicism and popular music through an 'explosion of confession and expression'.

Jana Bokova, a refugee from Czechoslovakia in 1968, who worked as a photographer in Paris before coming to London, was an associate of Radford's at the National Film School. Her initial interest was in making fantasy features, but she was diverted into documentary work, in part because of a desire to explore the kind of 'feature situations' which she saw in reality. Each documentary is in a sense a 'sketch for a bigger painting', and provides a much easier and quicker way of capturing reality than features. In one case she was looking for a Chekhov short story to make as a film, but came upon an old man who seemed to her to be very Chekhovian: 'It was better just to do the story of this old man.' Her documentary account of *Sunset People* comprises numerous genre scenes involving the survivors and casualties of the Hollywood dream, which would be difficult to recreate as fiction. A former photographer, she is less concerned with words and dialogue than with images, atmosphere and 'visual dialogue – what people don't say but express through what we see of them'.

39

Other directors who came into features through documentaries include David Drury, the director of *Forever Young*. He was an editor before making a film on Alan Minter's failed attempt to regain the middleweight crown, which won him a prize at the Chicago Film Festival and the attention of David Puttnam. Pat O'Connor made around eighty documentaries for the Irish network Radio Telefis Eireann (RTE) before directing the film dramas *Ballroom of Romance* and *One of Ourselves* for the BBC, and making his feature début with *Cal*. O'Connor describes his documentary work as an 'effort to express myself which didn't have much to do with traditional documentary'. Bill Forsyth also worked in documentaries prior to making *That Sinking Feeling, Gregory's Girl, Local Hero* and *Comfort and Joy*: 'It was useful not for the subject matter but just for the use of film, because it was a way of learning and working with film.'

During the 1970s and early 1980s the development of television drama and documentary was enriched by the arrival of the first graduates from the National Film School. Apart from Radford and Bokova, there was Nick Broomfield, who directed the feature-length documentaries *Soldier Girls* and *Chicken Ranch* before developing some feature projects; and Malcolm Mowbray, whose direction of the Alan Bennett play *Our Winnie* for the BBC secured him a commission to do Bennett's *A Private Function* as a feature. There are many other NFS-trained directors who have brought to the television companies a knowledge of cinema history, an understanding of the techniques of film-making and a perception of the capabilities of the medium far beyond television's inherent grasp of such things.

Whereas various other film schools concentrate on the technical processes of film-making, or on helping those with a background in the fine arts to develop a personal approach to film-making, the National Film School was founded to prepare students to play a dominant role in the commercial film industry. Students are selected not only for their creative talents, but also for a willingness to initiate projects and to fit into the mainstream of British cinema, however that is currently defined. The school is, as its director Colin Young acknowledges, better at turning out extremely competent film-makers than at nurturing the individual voice.

When Nicolas Roeg served on the selection panel, he felt that there was a tendency at the point of entry to pass over the oddball film-maker in favour of students who could fit easily into the structures and programmes of the school. In so far as it is directors, writers, producers and others from a relatively conservative film and television industry who select the students, and then play a major part in directing their efforts while at the school, the charge may be a fair one. Further, as the school gains prestige within the industry and becomes increasingly sophisticated in training students, the pressure develops to deprive students of opportunities to be spontaneous and pursue diverse paths. Michael Radford, who was among one of the first intakes to the school, claims to have found the fact that he was left substantially to his own devices in making his two school films very stimulating: 'It gave me the confidence to believe in my own ideas, along with a quality control over elements such as sound, camera and production.' Brian Gilbert, a more recent graduate from the school, argues that students can still enjoy that freedom if they desire it. He feels that the increasing conservatism in the films produced is not the result of the pressures exerted by the teachers: 'The restrictions on stylistic innovation tend to be self-imposed. The fact is that the students know that if they don't make a movie which will sell their talent, they are not using the film school properly. It is a sort of inner Geiger counter. It is inevitable.'

The shadow of the graduation screenings where student work is put on display for the industry and recent graduates anxiously seek out work looms large over the school's activities. Someone who makes a highly experimental work knows that the school is unlikely to present it to the industry punters. Colin Young, who observes that 'finally it is your fantasies that are going to sustain you, no matter how skilled you've become' is aware of the problem and looking for new ways of encouraging students to be outrageous and icono-clastic in their approach to film. One possible course, which would be largely invisible to the outside world, is to increase the use of video and to encourage all students to make competent but throwaway productions: 'That way, we'll be able to lower the costs of the exercise and encourage them to take risks and be more ambitious.'

Although students in the art colleges have also come under pressure to produce work that will attract the atten-tion of prospective employers, the tendency within insti-tutions such as the Royal College of Art is to encourage experimentation and the development of a distinctive per-sonal approach to film-making. Until the advent of Channel Four, however, the work of film-makers working within the fine arts tradition was made with such minimal resources, and with such a ghetto mentality, that it was practically invisible both to audiences and to more conventionally oriented film-makers. The choice presented to the art school film graduate has been between adapting to the conventions of film and television drama, or remaining as closet artists without any means of address to the mainstream.

The career of James Scott illustrates the dilemma. He was trained as an artist at the Slade, but was never tempted to emulate the career of his father, William, as a painter. His directorial début was *The Rocking Horse*, a short film made in 1962 with finance from the British Film Institute (BFI). It explored the *angst* of a young biker who takes to the streets in the search for fun, but when he finds it in the bed of an exotic painter, feels threatened by the girl's sophistication and aloofness. Scott was invited to make a film for Tony Richardson at Woodfall Films, but declined because he found himself out of tune with the concerns of Free Cinema and the structure of commercial film-making at the time. In the twenty years between *The Rocking Horse* and his Oscar-winning short, *A Shocking Accident*, he made two low-budget features, *Adult Fun* and *Coilin and Platonida*, documentaries on such artists as Richard Hamilton, R. B. Kitaj and David Hockney, and involved himself with the politically radical Berwick Street Collective in their production of the documentary, *Nightcleaners*.

Peter Greenaway was another director who took a long time to come to wide public attention. He graduated from the Walthamstow School of Art in the mid-1960s and eked out a living as a film editor for the government-sponsored Central Office of Information, while making numerous short films using his own resources. The British Film Institute eventually stepped in to fund *A Walk Through H*, *The Falls* and his first relatively commercial feature, *The Draughtsman's Contract*. Greenaway continued to draw and write throughout this period.

Other British directors who have emerged from a fine arts background include Phil Mulloy, a graduate from the Royal College of Art, who followed his didactic historical feature, *In the Forest*, with a more subtle documentary for the Arts Council on Bloomsbury artist *Mark Gertler*. He has since made the hour-long drama, *Souvenirs*, for Channel Four. Edward Bennett came from the same school, and his BFI-funded *Ascendancy* won the Berlin Festival Golden Bear in 1983. Bill Douglas secured a place at the London Film School with his drawings and then went on to explore his intellectually deprived upbringing in a Scottish mining village through his autobiographical film trilogy. Derek Jarman started making movies on Super 8mm while working as an art director on Ken Russell's *The Devils* and *Savage Messiah*. He has continued to paint and work in video while attempting to raise money from an unsympathetic industry for projects to follow up his first three low-budget features, all distinguished by their visual panache and sense of design.

For most British directors the road to features is a hard one, involving a long stay in various training areas and it is rare for a relative novice to get an opportunity to handle the length and the weight of a feature film. Bill Forsyth did manage to put together his dark comedy, *That Sinking Feeling*, with minimal resources and a lot of goodwill at a time when his career as a documentarist had hit an all time low. Colin Gregg, who initially worked in theatre, has skilfully juggled various packages of television money to make three feature-length films – *The Trespasser, Remembrance* and *To the Lighthouse* – after making two shorter items. Chris Petit also managed to tack together a budget of £80,000 from British and German sources for his directorial début, *Radio On*, after working as a script reader for Warner Brothers and a film critic for *Time Out* magazine. He then obtained commercial funding for his £800,000-budgeted adaptation of the P. D. James crime thriller *An Unsuitable Job for a Woman*, which was neither sufficiently arty for the arthouse audience, nor accessible enough for mass audiences to make him a safe bet for financiers. However, with the help of the BFI, Channel Four and Wim Wenders's Road Movies company, he financed his mystery thriller, *Flight to Berlin*.

In the past twenty years, the parlous condition of the British film industry has also effectively closed off opportunities for technicians in other areas of the film production process to try their hand at directing. Editors such as David Gladwell, the director of *Requiem for a Village* and *Memoirs of a Survivor*, and Kevin Brownlow, described by Mamoun Hassan as 'one of the most gifted film-makers that this country has got', on the basis of *It Happened Here*, and his intense English civil war polemic, *Winstanley*, have seemed to lack the persistence and willingness to compromise necessary to develop a career in features. Brownlow is also a historian of silent cinema, making the *Hollywood* and *Unknown Chaplin* series for Thames Television, as well as restoring Abel Gance's *Napoleon*, and presenting such silent classics as *The Crowd, Flesh and the Devil* and *The Wind* to successive London Film Festival audiences.

Andrew Birkin did manage to graduate from menial film

industry activities through screenwriting to the status of
feature director. He was assistant director on Stanley
Kubrick's science fiction epic *2001*, before joining David
Puttnam and Sandy Lieberson in the VPS/Goodtimes com-
pany, where he gained scriptwriter credits on *The Pied
Piper, Melody* and *Inside the Third Reich*. He wrote *The
Lost Boys*, a BBC television series based on his own bio-
graphy of J. M. Barrie and, while writing the script for *The
Final Conflict – Omen III*, and directing his short film,
*Sredni Vashtar*, secured a three-picture writing-directing
deal with Paramount Pictures. His feature début *The Cement
Garden*, an adaptation of Ian McEwan's short novel about
the unhappy fantasies of an adolescent boy, will be
made by Virgin Films. Birkin comments on his slow climb to
the director's chair: 'It's the only profession where you
spend twenty-five years as an apprentice, never doing the
thing that you hope finally to do – directing.'

Despite the diversity in the origins and ambitions of those
directors who made their first features in the early 1980s,
women and ethnic film-makers have yet to make their mark
on British cinema. It is possible that the activity of the
National Film School in training members of both groups
will eventually change that situation. Women have in fact
occasionally been in the majority of any year's entrants to
the NFS, and the fact that they have not found the opportunity to make films for television or cinema is testimony to
the deep conservatism that still imbues many quarters of the
commercial industry, rather than to any lack of confidence
on the part of the film-makers concerned. Colin Young
observes that female graduates have found it easier to pin
down jobs as writers than as directors, and women are to be
found in every other sector of the industry.

The only women who directed British films in 1983 were
Zelda Barron, an experienced continuity supervisor, who
worked on both Warren Beatty's *Reds* and Barbra Streisand's
*Yentl* prior to directing *Secret Places*; and Christine Edzard,
who made the small-scale but innovative *Biddy*, an evo-

45

cation of the life of a Victorian nanny. NFS graduates with features in the offing include Jana Bokova, whose *Hôtel du Paradis* centres on the annual trips to Paris made by a failed actor; Conny Templeman, who has money from the National Film Finance Corporation for her feature, *Nanou*; and Jenny Wilkes, who attracted the attention of David Puttnam with her graduation film, *Mother's Wedding*. Clare Peploe is another active woman director who will follow her Oscar-nominated short film, *Couples and Robbers*, with *Taramasalata*, a comic feature exploring various misunder tandings that develop between a group of art collectors and tourists gathered on a Greek island.

The situation is less positive for black film-makers. Horace Ove has worked only in television since making his feature, *Pressure*, with finance from the BFI. Menelik Shabbazz received funding from the same source for *Burning an Illusion*, an accessible account of the politicization of a young black woman whose boyfriend is unjustly arrested. 'Black film-makers,' suggests Shabbazz, 'have a lot to say and a lot of new things to say, which people will only come to realize in time. As far as I am concerned the current film culture doesn't really have much to say, and is dying. I haven't seen any white film-makers who are able to speak to mass audiences and deal with average normal situations, working-class situations.'

Ultimately, no training ground can do more than give a director the technical means to realize his personal view of the world. While work in documentaries and television drama may enable a director to fully develop a latent vision, those who embark upon a first career in commercials or pop promos as a stepping stone to features, must be sure of their vision if they are to emerge from their training with ideas on which to exercise their personal facility. A protracted edu cation in the techniques of film is the least important re quirement for the acquisition of a cinematic voice. When Neil Jordan made his first feature, *Angel*, his only experience of any audio-visual medium lay in a few film and television scripts which he had written, and the filming of a documentary on the making of John Boorman's *Excalibur*, a film on which he was credited as creative adviser. Nevertheless, *Angel* was described by one reviewer as 'the most accomplished feature début by an English-language film-maker this side of the Atlantic in years'. What he brought to his first film was a perspective on the world which he had developed in his fiction (*Night in Tunisia, The Past*), the sensitivities of an intelligent film viewer, and a clear sense of why he wanted to move into the film medium: 'The main attraction for me in making films is talking publicly about something, the attraction of composing a story out of familiar elements and out of things that will appeal to an audience, and developing it in more direct and broad strokes than I tended to in my fiction.' Others have entered more tentatively into film-making, with a creative strength derived from working in another medium – photography, literature, painting, theatre – whose potential they feel that they have fully explored.

It is only confidence in a strong personal vision that can sustain a director through the ups and downs that are an integral part of any career in features. The German director Werner Herzog was once present at a meeting held in the offices of the Association of Independent Producers (AIP) to discuss film industry training schemes. After listening to Colin Young talking about the possible form of a short course for producers, Herzog interjected that the film school should set up a boxing ring in which its students could develop their physical strength and moral fibre. Herzog's point, which he has expressed in other definitions of a director relating to a capacity to jump one's own height and walk from Paris to Munich, was that the only way to survive as a director is through personal resilience. The acquisition of the necessary skills, the money raising process, the nitty-gritty of production and the exposure of what one has made to the public gaze necessarily involve a lot of knocks. 'The greatest attribute of a director,' suggests Roger Christian, 'is to have the tenacity to hang on when your fingers are bleeding and you are crawling down the wall. Too many English directors just cave in, get one bad review and run moaning.' Without an inner certainty that you have a view of the world that is of value to other people, no amount of technical brilliance or stylistic pirouettes will be of any worth.

# 3

# AUDIENCES

Film-making is only occasionally a private art. In Britain at least there have been scant resources for those who want to make films that only develop an exclusively personal vision or intellectual theory. For the film-maker who seeks to find an audience the ambition is both to articulate a personal perspective and to find a way of communicating that world view to a larger public. A film-maker will redirect his immediate instinct towards making a film accessible and popular, according to his or her definition of the intended audience. The private film-maker's obscurantism expresses a demand that anyone who wants to understand a film must make the same journey as the film-maker. The arthouse film-maker anticipates only an audience drawn from an intelligent élite, which can respond to various artistic and intellectual references, and will make some effort to understand what is on the screen. But many of the new film-makers aspire to the condition of American cinema, which has found a way of communicating to a large popular audience internationally. The proviso is that they also seek to maintain a measure of personal and cultural integrity.

Reaching a definition of the target audience in the British context is especially difficult, because of the continuing shrinkage of the British cinema market. The re-creation of British cinema is seen as largely dependent on making films that will revive an enthusiasm for cinema in the British public, and in attracting new audiences. Television provides

49

no answers. The charge sometimes raised by those who work in television, that the very ambition to make cinema is élitist, just won't stick. It is of the essence of cinema, whether of the arthouse or popular variety, that it touches on universal themes and appeals to an audience undistinguished by nationality or class. Parochial issues are the stuff of television drama. Cinema is also concerned to offer a form of entertainment and intellectual satisfaction that transcends the necessary limitations of television drama. 'Cinema to me,' says Julien Temple, 'is a combination of everything – painting, writing, video – and I think it should be fought for tooth and nail. I'm proud that I haven't given in to do television plays, because it would sully and dirty that belief in cinema.'

A film-maker develops a public vision through dialogue with the audience, by exposing his own sentiments and waiting for the feedback. 'When you make a film,' says Nic Roeg, 'all you are really doing is saying: "This is the way I think, is there anyone out there?"' The hope is that if the vision is expressed with sufficient passion and confidence, it will be recognized and understood by those who see the film. As Derek Jarman expresses it: 'I make a film for myself and the thirty other people who work with me. I am not interested in what is commercial. If the audience want to be interested in me that is their business.' Bill Douglas wrote his *Tolpuddle* script in the belief that the history of the Tolpuddle Martyrs would be of interest to a broad public, but also because he felt some identification with the characters in the story. Andrew Birkin, in writing the screenplay for *The Cement Garden*, believed that it would appeal to 'enough people with my slightly warped tastes who will want to go and see it. You make films for yourself, and what you hope is that there will be enough people who think like you to like it. I think that if you try and make a thing for an audience that is not yourself, then how on earth can you second-guess somebody that isn't you. It would be like trying to design a house for somebody who had competely different tastes to you. What's the point?'

The producer is in some sense the audience's representative during the film-making process. To fulfil that function, the producer must be able to find ways of making a film accessible, while still allowing the director the scope to express a personal vision. David Puttnam comments on his willingness to make compromises in the later stages of the production process: 'The day we start to cut the picture, what I care about is the way it will affect the people watching it. If I had to, I'd turn the whole picture upside down and sling magenta light through it if I thought it would be more effective and get its points across better.' However, Pat O'Connor, who directed *Cal* for Puttnam, testifies that the only pressure he felt from the producer concerned keeping his vision intact: 'There was no talk of my making a snazzy, upbeat, flash film. First of all, I'd be totally the wrong person to do it. Secondly, it wouldn't be possible to do it. The thing to do is to try and go for the truth of the story and to try and make it as interesting as possible. I don't want to make some obscure pile of rubbish that nobody understands, but I want to make the film I want to make.'

Even in the relatively non-commercial film-making area, it is possible for the producer to introduce elements that will make a film more accessible. Peter Sainsbury, head of the British Film Institute Production Board, has encouraged film-makers working with BFI finance to cast their scripts within a narrative structure, use well-known names in the cast, and employ skilled technicians to secure the highest production values possible with a low budget. Sainsbury's aim to maximize the audience for films which are innovative in their use of the film medium has brought strong criticism from experimental film-makers who interpreted such measures as attempts to compromise a director's creative integrity. Such criticisms spring from a deep disdain for the audience and a refusal to take any steps towards accessibility. As Peter Greenaway, who made *The Draughtsman's Contract* with BFI funds, remarks: 'Some people might say that they're making films before their time and that it will all happen in ten or twenty years, but the cinema will be dead by then, so there isn't any point.'

The significance of a film depends on the vision that it expresses. Where a film's starting point is an analysis of the audience, which determines its subject and style, the result can only be vapid commercial pap. 'If the banner is entertainment,' argues Mamoun Hassan, 'then you end up with distraction. If the banner is something else, then you make it entertaining because you want the audience to see it.' Within the initial vision, there should be room to consider ways of finding a clearer articulation of the film's message. Many producers and executives testify to a greater willingness on the part of the new British film-makers to find ways of addressing an audience and making commercial films. According to Sandy Lieberson, head of production at Gold-crest Films, 'they are less professionally principled, more interested in making movies and commercial films rather than using the cinema as a platform to express their ideologies'. Al Clark of Virgin Films also testifies to a 'decline in the form of directorial self-regard, where the objective of getting done what you want is so out of sync with the thinking about who's going to go and see it that the result is zero takings at the box office. The departure point should always be the people, in whatever numbers it's scaled to, who will want to go and see it. You don't make it so impenetrable or so private that the prospect of reaching any audience at all is eliminated.'

The opportunity for the different approaches of director and producer or executive to find a meeting point can only exist when there is a shared appreciation of the audience. Too often British film executives have confused their desire to make commercial movies with a patronizing view of the audience that discounts their capacity to appreciate any sophistication of imagery and ideas – a course that can only lead to films that are crass and banal. For most of the new film-makers, the chief concern is that the doors be kept open so that they are given a chance to find an audience for their films. They do not, for the most part, want to make arthouse movies for small élite audiences, yet they are also unwilling to make anonymous and banal commercial films. They seek the right to experiment and challenge the audience. Bill Douglas comments that, 'there's nothing wrong with the audiences, and I never felt that there was. I think they're more intelligent than sometimes people might think. They just need to be helped towards taking in something else.' Nicolas Roeg argues in a similar vein: 'They might not like the things, but that's something different. People understand things. It's difficult enough to understand each other. We mumble and stumble onwards, but we read each other and figure things out.' Peter Greenaway observes that, however complex the frames of reference brought to a film by a film-maker and however seemingly arcane, there will often be ways for the audience to understand what is happening. Surrealism, for example, may not be known as a movement to many people, yet as a form of communication it is plastered across every advertising billboard in the country: 'Walking up and down London's Piccadilly, you'll see thousands of images which owe their origin to surrealist painting. So, to a much lesser extent other forms of painting aesthetic have filtered down to our general experience.'

Cinema can be extremely innovative and adventurous, but still reach out to popular audiences, simply because, to a greater or lesser degree, its products appeal to the emotions. Whereas television drama has to be directly understood, cinema can evoke an instinctive response and appeal to subconscious ways of knowing. The best films are designed to be felt, and then understood. James Scott shares the feeling that 'many of the ideas that people have about what the popular audience understands are complete bullshit.' He recognizes that cinema 'is a popular medium, and if you want to spend millions of pounds you cannot do it on a personal whim. One is in the business of entertainment and it has got to be shocking or terrifying, or just make people sit up, not just an intellectual exercise.' Nevertheless, he points

53

out that the visually unsophisticated subjects of the radical documentary *Nightcleaners*, which made use of such experimental devices as black spacing between images, not only appreciated the film but formulated their own sensible explanations for the form chosen by the film-makers. Jeremy Thomas observes that 'everybody understands a film at the level on which they can understand a film. Everybody's perception of a problem or a fact is different. When you look at a painting you get different things out of it. You just hope that other people get out of a film what you are getting out of it. Maybe there are many more things that they are getting than you realize were there. Whenever you show a film to an audience, you find the questions asked afterwards bring out a whole Pandora's box of what exactly is going on there.'

The challenge of commercial film-making is to find a form that exploits the richness of the film medium to create a multi-layered and open-ended film, which can be understood on a simple narrative plane but also yields up richer levels to those willing to search for them. The ultimate achievement, according to Mamoun Hassan, lies in making 'films of substance for the largest audience, and popular films with serious undertones that are about something – not pap that makes money or arthouse movies that few people will see'. Alan Parker says: 'I am not interested in a film to be shown at a small cinema to a small group of people. Far from inhibiting me, it is the reason why I want to make films. We have got to learn to communicate.' Puttnam argues that 'the very factor in cinema that was seen to be its limitation has turned out to be its greatest creative challenge, which is that because of the costs, you need a lot of people to see it.'

Such pragmatic attitudes might seem to require a compromise of creative ambition, but it only requires an intelligent act of subversion to smuggle original, striking and complex ideas into a form that is relatively conventional and easily accessible. At its simplest level, this may only involve counterpointing scenes that challenge and provoke an audience against the visual pleasures offered by 'chocolate box' elegance. The genres of the crime thriller and science fiction adventure provide a film-maker with a set of conventions that are understood, and within which it is possible to explore a personal vision. David Puttnam often finds himself looking for stories in sport and popular music, because within those universally understood lifestyles and values it is possible to spin metaphors that explore more profound ideas. To work in such a way requires both a confidence in your own vision, and an acceptance that much of the audience will miss some layers in the message. For Andrew Birkin, the capacity of a film to work on two planes is one of the pleasures of film-making. He says that it wouldn't sadden him if eighty per cent of the audience didn't catch what a film was saying: 'I hope it is working on a more straightforward level. It is very rewarding even if only a few people realize what you are actually up to.'

Puttnam considers that one of the mistakes made by film-makers of the 1970s was their simplistic view that to convey a message, you had to take a heavy-handed and didactic stance: 'If you made a left wing film, you made it in terms that only a left wing person would ever want to watch. We weren't very clever, we weren't subversive enough.' He points to East European cinema as an indication of a way in which messages can be communicated more subtly through metaphor: 'I always loved the idea that the Czech film, *Closely Observed Trains*, was banned by the Russians three years after it was released because they suddenly realized that it wasn't really about the Nazis, it was about them, by which time it had won an Academy Award and everything else. I think that is fantastic and that is what we haven't been doing.' There are powerful political films which convey their message in a direct way. Pontecorvo's *The Battle of Algiers* and Joffe's *The Killing Fields* are key examples. Both are films which represent epic historical events and articulate attitudes which are broadly understood and accepted. Where the subject is less thrilling and the point of the view has less appeal to the consensus, the film-maker must adopt a more devious path.

It is essential for a film-maker's confidence in his vision that his or her film should be understood by somebody. Bill Forsyth's description of himself as a serious-minded and didactic film-maker to some extent belies his public image. He worries that he may have been too sophisticated, when he considers the extent to which both critics and fellow film-makers seem to have missed the serious elements in his films, including *Local Hero*: 'There's a lot of ironic comment in there which seems to have passed people by. Maybe it is just too underplayed in the script. The way I was trying to make it work was that the more low key it was, the more pene-trating it would be, but obviously it doesn't work. Maybe people don't want to have to give that kind of attention to something. Maybe you have to be broad and dramatic or something. It is amazing how crude you have to be in a film.'

The statements made by the new British film-makers about the need to make commercial films which will appeal to a popular audience are often simplistic, and sometimes self-contradictory. There is a tendency to skate over the difference between a visually sophisticated and intellectually complicated arthouse movie, and a film that relies upon action and adventure to convey its message. The relative confusion from which these remarks emerge reflects upon the dire state of cinema exhibition in Britain, and the fear that the television screen will shortly become the only outlet for audiovisual productions. In 1981 David Puttnam wrote: 'I make films for people to see. If I have a message to convey, I should convey it in whatever form the audience prefers to see it. In Britain the audience has an expressed preference to see my work on television.' Many in the film industry read the remark as a sign of defeatism, a fact which caused Puttnam some chagrin: 'The frustrating thing about this country is that your view becomes synonymous with your desire. I wish people went to the cinema. I wish they went three times a week. I wish the cinemas were great. I always rather hoped that, by drawing attention to what was happening, it would give us a better chance of trying to retain cinemas.'

There is no doubt about the British hunger for movies. With about 6 million video-cassette recorders in British homes, and brightly-decorated video shops on nearly every High Street, even in remote Welsh villages, Britain leads the world in its enthusiasm for video in the same way that it once set the international record for cinema-going. In 1950 the average cinema attendance per person for the year was twenty-eight visits, as compared to twenty-three in the US and less than twenty in the rest of the world. In no other country has the penetration of video-recorders into the market been so rapid or thorough as in Britain. By contrast, a quarter of the British population no longer has a cinema within 20 miles of its home, and a mere 70 million cinema tickets were sold in British theatres in 1983 (1,400 million in 1950). Yet, people did pack the cinemas to see *Chariots of Fire* and *Local Hero*, and the London arthouses were full when they showed *The Ploughman's Lunch* and *The Draughtsman's Contract*. For British film-makers attempting to develop the aesthetics of cinema, and to stir again in audiences an enthusiasm for the cinema experience, the facts present a depressing, if perplexing, prospect.

The extent of the decline in cinema-going, and the shrinkage of the cinema network (the main circuits operated only 202 theatres at the end of 1983), is unique to Britain. In the US, despite the growth of cable television services offering round-the-clock movie programmes, cinema audiences have expanded in recent years. In various European countries, cinemas have been maintained and developed thanks to judicious government intervention, sensible managements and, in France at least, a steady flow of native films. In Britain, where there has been no system of subsidy for cinemas, the dominant power exerted by the two major cinema circuits, Rank and EMI, has gradually strangled the health of the exhibition sector. The patterns of exhibition are finely tuned to maximize the market for major American films such as *Return of the Jedi*, *Flashdance* or *Octopussy*, but leave no space for the intelligent distribution of smaller entertainments – from a European comedy to a low-budget American horror picture or a British film. The excitement of the cinema-going experience has now been largely destroyed by the transformation of medium-sized halls into cheapskate mini-theatres which offer audiences little opportunity for communal experience. To a considerable extent audiences have not opted for domestic entertainment in place of cinema, they have simply been driven away from the cinemas.

The British film production industry must shoulder some of the blame for the decline in cinema-going. It has consistently failed to generate a flow of films that would speak to British audiences in a stimulating way about their own cultural and social context. The minimal revenues now available to British producers from the home market show the size of the problem that must be solved to assure a long-lasting revival in production activity. The epic *Gandhi* managed to take around £2,500,000 from the British market in 1983, a performance which rivalled that of such films as *Octopussy* and *Return of the Jedi*. *Local Hero* grossed around £500,000, and such medium-budget pictures as *Educating Rita* and *Heat and Dust* took a decent £300,000, while films like *Scrubbers, The Return of the Soldier* and *Party Party* scarcely managed to collect £100,000. Such a figure represents not only a tiny fraction of a film budget, but is scarcely enough to pay the costs of distribution. The films financed by Channel Four which were distributed in the same period, such as *Another Time, Another Place, The Draughtsman's Contract* and *The Ploughman's Lunch*, were in an even worse position because, while they took good money in London's prestige arthouse cinemas, they were ostracized from any of the circuit cinemas which operate an embargo on any films set to play on television within three years of their theatrical release.

Much of the decline in cinema-going internationally is the result of the development of television. With the emergence of cable, video and various other systems for feeding images into the home, it is clear that cinema will never again play the role in people's lives that it did in the post-war years. Nevertheless, cinema does provide audiences with a valuable communal experience and unique forms of pleasure. For film-makers, it is the only canvas that fully challenges their creative resources. The cinema circuits, in their inability to find ways of encouraging the production and dissemination of British films, have been their own worst enemy. The healthiest cinema market in Europe is France, where fifty per cent of admissions are for local product. While audiences everywhere will turn out for the latest heavily promoted spectacle from Hollywood, a genuine interest in cinema on the part of an audience has to be founded on a steady flow of, perhaps smaller, films which reflect the audience's own cultural and social concerns. This does not necessarily mean films have to be about Britain but that they see the world, life and culture within a British context.

It is just possible that the development of new forms of distribution will be the saving of cinema. Both Rank and EMI now recognize that there is an increase in the demand internationally for 'software' to feed the new distribution systems, and that cinemas provide the ideal showcase from which new films can be launched into other media and markets. In parallel with its increased interest in producing medium-budget British films, Thorn EMI has taken steps to improve the quality of the management at its cinemas; to increase the range of the films shown on its screens; and to upgrade those cinemas still in operation. Rank Films has been investing to secure rights in British feature films, while trying to make space on its screens not only for a range of low-budget British movies, but also for smaller European and American films which have less than mass appeal.

The increasing risk involved in releasing any film to British cinemas has gradually restricted the range of productions which distributors have been willing to show. The video market, however, has provided a risk cushion for those handling such films, and has been exploited by various distribution companies to make new types of film available to British audiences. Unlike the older arthouse distributors who have tended to rely exclusively upon the London market to secure revenue for European films, Palace Pictures sought to maximize the penetration of the French film, *Diva*, not only through the use of circuit cinemas outside the metropolis, but also by simultaneous release on video. The same strategy was employed with even greater success for Nagisa Oshima's *Merry Christmas, Mr Lawrence*, a film which might otherwise have been relegated to mere arthouse status. Like Virgin Films, which released the horror spoof *Eating Raoul* as well as the cultish American independent picture, *Liquid Sky*, Palace's target audience is sophisticated youth, a group which is not adequately catered for by the mass release films. It is an area which both companies are exploring in their film production policies. 'To make a film,' suggests Virgin's Al Clark, 'which isn't just a "youth" movie, but has a range of elements which are just automatically attractive to that age group is very appealing.' Julien Temple, whose understanding of youth culture has been heightened by his work in pop promos, believes that if more effort was made to tap the young market, 'the whole fabric of the cinema as we know it could change rapidly. There is an audience that hasn't been fed into. A few films that hit that could change the structure of the whole thing overnight.'

An intelligent strategy, whereby cable and video are used to stimulate British film production and broaden the range of films distributed to British cinemas, could bring about a revival of cinema-going. There are no guarantees of success. Producers and executives must recognize that cinema provides the maximum challenge to a film-maker's creative powers. Directors must seize that challenge and create work that is accessible and popular. 'Everybody,' says Al Clark, 'has got to get into a barricade-storming mood about it, and producers and exhibitors should realize that they have a crisis in common, which has to be resolved in common.'

# 4

---

# MONEY

The vitality of a film culture depends on its diversity. If a film industry concentrates on producing large-budget movies aimed at the international market, it will offer few opportunities for untested directors and innovative film ideas. If the industry does not have the ambition to transcend the limitations of the local market, its products are likely to become stale and inward looking. The health of the whole production sector is dependent on the evolution of new forms and fresh styles. In any area of production, there must be a range of competing companies to which film-makers can apply for funds, each allotting their resources according to different criteria of selection. Too often in the past, the lure of the American market has tempted British production companies to direct all their energies towards major films. In the late 1960s and 1970s, when American audiences and executives appeared to be indifferent towards British movies, and television companies refused to compensate for the decline in the local cinema market by funding British film production, the industry was in the worst of all possible worlds. The revival of the early 1980s was made possible by two developments: a renewal of US interest in British projects, initiated by the success of *Chariots of Fire* and further stimulated by the broadening of the American market as a consequence of the development of cable television; and the setting up of Channel Four, the first British television channel with an interest in financing low-budget films. Combined with the development of the video market and the distant prospect of British cable television, these factors were sufficient to generate finance for a broad range of film productions.

There is constant pressure on British producers to 'go American' and throw into one superproduction money sufficient to pay for twenty smaller films. Whereas European producers also long to penetrate the US market, the largest and wealthiest in the world, they have generally attempted to maintain their cultural integrity. British producers consider that they speak the same language as the Americans and have cherished the fond illusion that if they made films according to 'formulas' which worked for American films they could secure a parallel success in the international market-place. While many directors, producers and technicians were lured across the Atlantic to escape a moribund industry, the executives left behind often chose to make commercial pap that might pass as American. This short-sighted decision diverted them from producing low to medium-budget productions. Such films could not only exploit the revenue available from the British and European markets, but could also sow the seed for a new and vital British film industry, which in time might secure success in wider international markets. Quick solutions have generally been preferred to sensible long-term planning.

The fact that there was a British film industry to revive in the early 1980s owed little to American money or the production policies of the finance companies operating in the previous period. Its existence was due to the efforts of a few producers, and under-financed institutions, to make authentically British films. The work of the National Film School and other training institutions was also a contributing factor. Despite minimal resources, the British Film Institute Production Board and the National Film Finance Corporation provided creative opportunities for such directors of stature as Bill Douglas, Bill Forsyth, Chris Petit and Peter Greenaway, as well as others who have yet to reach creative maturity. Equally important were such producers as Clive Parsons, Don Boyd and David Puttnam, each of whom raised film budgets against formidable odds and promoted the careers of new film directors and writers.

By contrast, the production policies initiated in the 1970s by Barry Spikings at EMI and Lew Grade at ACC, which failed even to provide opportunities for those British directors so skilfully exploited by the American companies, seem totally irrelevant. The production programmes of both these executives involved international stars, and American or 'international' themes, and came to spectacular ends. Spikings had one success with Michael Cimino's *The Deerhunter*, against which he had to set losses on such pictures as *Can't Stop the Music* and *Honky Tonk Freeway*. Grade, whose tastes were some way down-market from those of Spikings and more 'international' in flavour, only hit gold with the American pictures *Sophie's Choice* and *On Golden Pond* after he had lost his position as chairman of the ACC Board due to the failure of such films as *Raise the Titanic* and *Green Ice*. These executives made a double misjudgement. They chose to make films outside a familiar production environment, and to participate with some enthusiasm in the current Hollywood mania for huge-budget pictures, resulting in equally huge losses when audiences showed no interest in the films.

The dilemma confronting British directors who had the opportunity to go to Hollywood in the 1970s was a difficult one. The state of the native industry left them with no choice but to accept the invitation, but the environment in Los Angeles was not necessarily the most creative one. The imaginative large-scale visions of a director such as Ridley Scott (*Blade Runner, Legend*) could perhaps only have been achieved in the Hollywood context, but this was not the case for those with more social and personal concerns. While Alan Parker claims that working in Hollywood implies no compromises in terms of subject matter, the aggression in his attacks on the mediocrity of the new British cinema seems to suggest a certain frustration at not being able to express a personal vision. In defending his films he emphasizes their achievements in photography and craft, rather than content. Peter Yates (*Breaking Away, The Janitor, Krull*) settled in New York and did find subjects within American life to which he could relate, but only reached his creative peak when he came back to London to make *The Dresser*. More recently, the films made for the American studios by British directors such as Roger Christian's *The Sender*, Franc Roddam's *The Lords of Discipline*, John MacKenzie's *The Honorary Consul* and Tony Scott's *The Hunger*, have aroused none of the excitement vouchsafed to film-makers working in Britain.

The problem for the British *émigrés* is not that of making films within a culture that is alien – there is no reason why British directors should not make fascinating films on American society – but that of working for companies that are less than sympathetic to new ideas. To submit to the abrasiveness of the Hollywood system and to resist the pressures to modify the original film concept because of some market analysis of audience requirements, requires a toughness and sense of inner certainty that only those who are bred to it can really possess. Roger Christian went through the 'nasty' experience of seeing his version of *The Sender* butchered by Paramount Pictures so that it could be sold as an exploitation picture and then dumped on to the market with minimal publicity. He describes the typical reaction of American distributors to the script of his new film, *2084*: 'What genre is this picture? It is not *Flashdance*, it is not *Return of the Jedi*, it is not James Bond. It has got androids in it, but it is not *Blade Runner*, because that didn't make money, so it must be *Star Wars*. Therefore, it has got to be made for the youth market, so we have to make the leads like this and alter the script in this way. There is no thought that the story actually works and that this is a different vision. If I went with a major, they would alter it until they got it into a flaccid floppy genre picture, and then they would say that it wasn't as good as *Star Wars* and kill it.' The fact that they are spending such large sums of money forces Hollywood executives to justify their investment by seeking to ensure that each picture imitates the last success despite the fact that the really successful picture is generally the first one in a thematic cycle. Andrew Birkin recalls asking a studio executive why he was backing *King David*, a biblical film written by Birkin for the Australian director, Bruce Beresford. He replied: 'We see it as a tale fitting into an archetypal pattern, with King David as Luke Skywalker, King Saul as Lord Darth Vader and the prophets Samuel and Nathan as Ben Kenobi, the wise man.' As a self-justificatory game, such remarks have their value, but when they are allowed to intrude into the process of developing an original human story, they can be very inhibiting. Birkin summarizes the studio dilemma: 'They hate the outrageous and they feel slightly ashamed of the bland. They want something very original for which there is a predestined place on the shelf.'

It goes against the grain for an American studio to finance a foreign picture. Ned Tanen, the former head of Universal Pictures, has described the interest taken by American companies in British movies during the early 1960s as a temporary aberration, resulting from the fact that too many executives had been dazzled by the bright lights of swinging London: 'The appeal of the subjects is not wide enough. They are viewed as provincial movies. The audience perceives them as "above" it in some way. It is very tough to sell a serious movie. When that serious movie is also relatively provincial it is doomed.' Nevertheless, a number of 'sophisticated' British movies did secure American financing in the early 1980s. David Puttnam built upon his success with *Chariots of Fire*, which demonstrated that a British director could handle a seemingly 'provincial' subject in a way that gave it universal impact, and raised money from Warner Brothers to develop numerous scripts and partially to fund, along with Goldcrest Films, Bill Forsyth's *Local Hero*, Roland Joffe's *The Killing Fields* and Pat O'Connor's *Cal*.

Goldcrest itself secured commitments from US distributors to several films made by directors who had already established a reputation in Hollywood. These included Peter Yates's *The Dresser* and John Boorman's *The Emerald Forest*, later abandoned by Goldcrest. The company's founder, Jake Eberts, considered that it was financially irresponsible to embark upon any major project without having secured a commitment from an American distributor: 'Leaving the US market until you have finished the film just doesn't make sense, because you leave the greatest amount of exposure against the largest potential market. If you fail to get your film into that market there is no way you can get your money back.' When the Canadian Eberts left Goldcrest in late 1983 to set up a parallel British production programme for the US distributor, Embassy Pictures, the American Sandy Lieberson took over production for the company.

Various other companies also emerged in the early 1980s which, while making films with a firm but intelligent eye on the American market, had much more flexibility than Goldcrest. They were willing to guarantee funds for quite substantially-budgeted pictures without necessarily securing advance interest from American distributors. Acorn pictures, set up by American businessman Herbert Oakes with equity financing from various city institutions, was responsible for two pictures directed by Lewis Gilbert: *Educating Rita* and *Not Quite Jerusalem*. *Rita* was sold for worldwide distribution to Columbia Pictures, but only after production had been completed. By not selling the picture in advance, Oakes says, 'you get a chance to place it with a distributor who is genuinely enthusiastic about what he has got, not what he hopes to get, and for whom the picture is genuinely important in the period that he hopes to release it'. Other advantages include the absence of any American pressure to modify the script in a negative direction, no pressure to use name artists who are not necessarily appropriate for the particular film, and the possibility of financial advantages, as the film may be a more valuable commodity when finished than it was as a concept. Another company with the same philosophy was HandMade Films, set up to make English comedies by an American, Denis O'Brien, and ex-Beatle George Harrison. Its films have included Terry Gilliam's *Time Bandits*, *Bullshot*, and *The Missionary*.

Outside the production departments of the major American distribution companies opportunities were opened up for British producers with the expansion of the American cable market. Not only did the largest cable supplier, Home Box Office, invest £1,400,000 in the budget of James Dearden's psychological thriller *The Cold Room*, but most of the American studios set up 'classics' distribution divisions. These subsidiary companies acquired European and American films which previously wouldn't have seen the light of a cinema screen in the USA, and gave them a theatrical showcase prior to their sale to cable. Orion Classics invested a small amount in Marek Kanievska's *Another Country*. It was United Artists Classics which arranged the American release of *The Draughtsman's Contract*, and Columbia's Triumph company handled Neil Jordan's *Angel*. An independent company run by Sam Goldwyn Jnr, which works to the same brief as the 'classics' outfits, bought Michael Radford's *Another Time, Another Place* as well as a batch of Goldcrest's smaller movies, including Peter Duffell's *Experience Preferred — But Not Essential*.

Together with some of the larger pictures that were handled by the main departments of the distribution companies, these films found an audience in America because they showed a degree of freshness and originality that contemporary American pictures could not match. As in the 1960s, American cinema was on one of its downward cycles, apparently preferring the crass and the gargantuan to the gentle and charming. As David Puttnam says of the American response to *Educating Rita*: 'It is a nicely directed, nicely acted "rites of passage" picture, produced in a period when that is the thing that they cannot do in American cinema without making it vulgar. Instead of being just a nice picture it becomes delightful, because the market is a bit of a desert at the moment.' For a period, at least, British films have established an identity as purveyors of an interesting and particular view of the world. 'Britain,' suggests Al Clark, 'is once again being seen as a place which, though the lustre has faded slightly, has a resilience, an originality and an imagination which is intrinsically attractive, even though some of its manifestations may not be.' He points to the parallel in the fortunes of various British rock groups which made a strong impact on the American scene in the early 1980s. Sandy Lieberson expresses the view that this wave of interest in British culture may be more enduring than that of the 1960s, thanks to the increased awareness of British culture and history which American youth has acquired through television shows like *Upstairs, Downstairs, Monty Python's Flying Circus* and such BBC output as is aired on public television.

It would, however, be rash to conclude that the increased acceptance of British films by US financiers and audiences is, in itself, an assurance of a healthy future for British film production. The American market is extremely conservative but nevertheless subject to changes in fashion. If British financiers become so dependent on the American market that it becomes impossible to make a film without either the say-so of an American distributor or a reasonable guarantee that it is something which American audiences will bite at, they will ignore the potential richness of British cinema. Goldcrest's achievement in arousing American interest in a handful of projects has to be seen in the context of the limitations imposed on the company by this approach. *Suicide – The Movie* had to be abandoned because of a lack of American enthusiasm. The company also had to remove Julien Temple after he had spent eighteen months working on the script of *Mandrake the Magician*, a magical fantasy based on an American comic strip character, because the US distributor, Embassy, became nervous about employing a novice director on the project. Warner Brothers may have shown an increasing enthusiasm for films made by David Puttnam, but every British film developed from the London base of its subsidiary, The Ladd Company, was denied the production green light. The promise that US cable and the 'classics' distributors will become the natural funding source for the sort of smallish middle-of-the-road movies which are a British forte could well turn sour if the companies start to compete for audiences with productions similar to the fare offered by the US network companies. According to Sandy Lieberson, the tide has already begun to turn: 'Cable is one of the most disappointing things that has happened in the past ten years. We all had such great hopes and expectations that it was going to be the outlet for really interesting and unusual films that may not have had a big enough cinema potential and that weren't ordinary enough for television, and yet it has gone the other way.'

For the moment, British films are riding high. It will only take a series of failures, however, to retard and damage the current healthy development in the Anglo-American relationship. It is essential that the British industry not only produces both large and small 'projects', but also develops a space for the production of films that play with new styles and fresh concepts. It takes time for a director to master the art of communicating his vision to an international audience, and the perception of many British film-makers derives from a European rather than an American perception of art and the world. To deny these facts, and to refuse to create a broadly-based British film industry, is to close the door to new talent, freshness and innovation.

During the 1970s, the state-backed National Film Finance Corporation should have been able to develop the possibilities for innovative film-making. It was, however, either managed in a pussyfooting way that involved no initiatives to carve out new areas in British film culture, or simply smothered by lack of funds. Mamoun Hassan, who took over the running of the Corporation in 1979, had a record of backing interesting projects while production head for the BFI's production arm. These included Bill Douglas's trilogy and Kevin Brownlow's *Winstanley*. He was unable to extend these initiatives at the NFFC. In the NFFC's 1979 annual report, Hassan defined the objectives of the Corporation: 'Resources are limited. There are other priorities than film-making. But most are agreed that film is essential as enter-tainment and culture, and therefore the Corporation's brief should be to make not only films that appeal to a popular audience but also films that feed ideas and invention. To attempt to separate these two aspects completely is to dis-courage the creation of a truly popular art.'

The British government is unique in Europe in its un-willingness to recognize that with the shrinking of the local cinema market, and the continued dominance of American films in that market, state intervention is required to stimulate production. The establishment of the Eady Levy in 1947 was a response to this fact. By allotting a portion of global box office receipts to British-made films, *pro rata* to each film's cinema performance, it sought to encourage British production and American investment in the British industry. By the mid-1970s, however, the levy system was in need of reform. The fund benefited major American pro-ductions which had been made in British studios, but did little to re-vitalize the local production sector. The Callaghan government had plans to establish a full system of state subsidy when it fell to Margaret Thatcher in 1979. The Conservative regime's meagre response to the film industry's plight was to allocate £1,500,000 annually from Eady to the NFFC.

The insufficiency of such funding, at a time when the rest of the industry was quiescent, affected the quality of works made by the NFFC. Despite the fact that there had been little opportunity to develop directorial skills, each director was under pressure to produce a major work. This was con-sidered the only way in which the government could be persuaded that the NFFC should be maintained. Such films as Franco Rosso's *Babylon*, David Gladwell's *Memoirs of a Survivor*, Chris Petit's *An Unsuitable Job for a Woman* and Lindsay Anderson's *Britannia Hospital* were all interesting, but not fully achieved, works. It was no accident that the NFFC's most commercially successful film, *Gregory's Girl*, was made in Scotland at the furthest remove from the NFFC's office, and called upon a smaller budget contribution from the Corporation than any of its other films. If a system of state assistance is to work effectively, it must ensure that it creates a sufficient base level of production to engender an atmosphere stimulating to creativity.

During Hassan's time at the NFFC, its capacity to effect any transformation of the film production sector was restricted by the relative absence of companies willing to co-invest on a regular basis with the Corporation. EMI was lured, somewhat against its nature, into *Memoirs of a Survivor* and *Britannia Hospital*. Goldcrest was cajoled by David Puttnam into investing in *An Unsuitable Job for a Woman* and later participated in Marek Kanievska's *Another Country*. Yet neither company was eager to establish a continuing relationship with the NFFC. It was only with the emergence of various new funding sources in 1983 that the NFFC was able to take a more effective stand within the industry. Indeed, it was largely due to support and advice from Hassan that the prosperous Virgin Records company was encouraged into film production, under the guiding hand of movie buff Al Clark. Virgin's intial partnership with the NFFC was on *A Shocking Accident*, an Oscar-winning short film produced by Christine Oestreicher and directed by James Scott. That was followed by co-investment in Richard Eyre's *Loose Connections* and Zelda Barron's *Secret Places*, the latter also involving such diverse bodies as Rank Film Distributors and Rediffusion Films, a subsidiary of the electronics company. Virgin has since gone on to invest in Michael Radford's *1984,* Steve Barron's *Electric Dreams* and Andrew Birkin's *The Cement Garden*.

The significance of Virgin for British film-makers is that,

alongside larger projects, the company is willing to consider films made on budgets of around £700,000 as sensible propositions. While allowing for high production values it is expenditure which may be recouped from European theatrical and television markets if the Americans fail to bite. There is, therefore, less pressure on producers to make any substantial concessions in the direction of American market acceptability. Like the Moving Picture Company, which announced a programme of low-budget pictures at the end of 1983, Virgin is a company with a sense of identity resulting from the fact that its production programme evolves from the instincts of executives rather than simple cost analysis and profit projections. The same cannot yet be said of the more anonymous sources of finance such as Rediffusion Films and United Media Finance, which have generally only contributed end money for projects initiated elsewhere. Al Clark defines the advantage of working at a relatively low-budget level: 'The subjects that you cover can often be more challenging and ultimately far more beneficial to the future of the cinema, in that they come from the imagination rather than from market research surveys. That contrasts with the Hollywood emphasis on thinking that it knows what the public wants, which is quite tiresome at best and thoroughly risible at worst, because it is completely illusory.'

With the freedom thus acquired, Virgin has been willing to take chances with new talent, introducing Andrew Birkin, Steve Barron, Zelda Barron and Paul Mayersberg to the rosters of British feature directors. It has also invested in short films by James Scott and Conny Templeman (*To Hell and Back in Time for Breakfast*) on the basis that someone has to 'take the initial risks so that the film-maker can be seen one way or another, and invest in people's careers, just to see what is going to flourish and what isn't'. Nevertheless, Virgin's production programme stops well short of any project which, in the judgement of its chief executives, has no commercial prospects. At script stage, that would probably have excluded such pictures as *Another Time, Another Place*, and *The Draughtsman's Contract*, which were financed respectively by Channel Four (with Rediffusion Films,) and the British Film Institute Production Board (with Channel Four).

The problem with a film like *The Draughtsman's Contract*, which was tightly budgeted at around £450,000 but appealed only to an arthouse audience, is that it is only the allocation of £150,000 to £200,000 from Channel Four that makes recoupment even a remote possibility. The lack of revenue from the UK theatrical market is a major stumbling block. In Britain, *The Draughtsman's Contract* showed at eighty-six venues prior to screening on television, but the money it took was barely sufficient to cover the cost of prints, distribution and promotion. It is possible that more theatrical money would have been made if the film had been screened in circuit cinemas, but then the Channel Four money would not have been available. The film was released across the USA with forty-five prints, but not until the film had grossed £2 million did the BFI start to recover anything over the £100,000 which it received as an advance for cable and theatrical rights. Advance payments from distributors in Italy, France, Germany and Scandinavia added up to about £120,000. 'At that point,' observes BFI production head, Peter Sainsbury, 'it starts getting difficult. It could just be that by the time all ancillary markets are sold off in the States and the European markets, we could over five years recoup our investment. Now that was a phenomenally successful film.' At the beginning of 1984, two years after completing work on *The Draughtsman's Contract*, Greenaway had several scripts ready to shoot, but none of them had attracted a promise of money from any source other than Channel Four.

In most European countries, but notably France and Germany, arthouse films are supported by a combination of government subsidy and television financing. In Britain, however, the government has never applied pressure to the television institutions to force them into making a commitment to an evolving film culture. The BFI has rarely had the resources to nurture the careers of individual film-makers; too often it has launched a new director, only to see his creative development curtailed through lack of support. Some relief for the sector has been offered since 1982 by Channel Four which, on the initiative of its chief executive, Jeremy Isaacs, decided to allocate the larger part of its drama budget to feature length films. This tied in with the Channel's mandate to work in areas not covered by the other commercial companies; to sponsor 'innovation' and 'experiment', and back the work of independent companies. The Channel has expressed an interest in the work of established arthouse directors such as Chris Petit (whose *Flight to Berlin* it part-funded), Derek Jarman and Bill Douglas, as well as launching the career of Neil Jordan, and has made an annual contribution to BFI funds. Nevertheless it has not fundamentally altered the situation for film-makers who cannot find funding in the commercial sector.

Although Channel Four's film policy is still evolving – positively, the main concern of the network's drama head, David Rose, has been to sponsor work for television, and the aesthetic values of most of the work made under its auspices are firmly rooted in television. With the exception of such films as Maurice Hatton's *Nelly's Version, Another Time, Another Place* and *Angel*, the preoccupation is with the telling of a straightforward narrative, rather than the creative use of film. 'Channel Four,' suggests Peter Sainsbury on the basis of the Channel's response to various projects which he has submitted, 'is not an adventurous spot for film-makers.' James Scott shares with many contemporary film-makers the view that the Channel's film output has been largely uninteresting as cinema: 'The films could have come from anywhere, even dropped from the moon. They don't relate to anything very much and show no awareness of cinema tradition.'

Despite the occasional crossing point, there is a wide

divergence between the objectives of Channel Four and those of the BFI. The BFI's brief, as defined by Sainsbury, is to: 'take artistic and aesthetic risks and demand the right to fail and make an awful picture, but all the time aspiring to make films that are not dull, which are exciting to look at, which have maximum production values for the budget available, and which are going to stretch people in one direction or another. We don't feel that there is any defensible future for us if we are only going to make feature-length television plays like the *First Love* series (made for Channel Four by Goldcrest).' Channel Four, on the other hand, allocated a large percentage of its programme commissioning budget (around £6 million in its first year) to a programme of twenty feature-length films, on the basis that the new movies might become the star attractions in its schedules. While the Channel is keen to win prestige by backing some arthouse films, the logic of economic survival is bound to dictate that more middle-of-the-road dramas such as Jack Gold's *Praying Mantis*, Gavin Millar's *Secrets* and Desmond Davis's *The Country Girls*, all of which secured high ratings, form the staple of its output.

Until the setting up of Film Four International in early 1984, the channel could not finance any film fully. Its general policy is to pay £200,000 for two transmissions of the production, invest another £100,000, and leave the producer to raise whatever else is required from another source. Bill Douglas's *Tolpuddle* project and Derek Jarman's *Caravaggio* both spent a long time at the starting blocks after receiving the promise of cash from Channel Four. Organizations such as Portman-Quintet Films, London Films Productions Ltd and Goldcrest Films and Television, which part-financed various films with Channel Four during its first eighteen months, are simply not interested in the more innovative film productions. The only alternative sources of cash are the European television companies, but there are few producers in Britain with any expertise in tapping these funds. German stations did put money into Chris Petit's

*Flight to Berlin* and Ken McMullen's *Ghost Dance*, but neither the French station FR3, which expressed an interest in Jana Bokova's *Hôtel du Paradis*, nor the Italian RAI network, which was going to invest in Jarman's *Caravaggio*, actually delivered.

Inspired by the example of Channel Four and an awareness of the prospective need for 'software' to supply the developing markets in cable, video and satellite, other British television companies have also shown an interest in putting money into feature film projects. The commercial companies have periodically attempted to set up subsidiaries which would make feature films for international markets – the most successful to date, ATV's Black Lion, was responsible for Ken Loach's *Looks and Smiles*, Stephen Frears's *Bloody Kids* and John MacKenzie's *The Long Good Friday* – but a tangle of tax regulations and union problems have always brought such ambitions to grief. Recent encouraging developments have included the creation of Zenith Productions as a feature finance arm of Central Television after the company had backed *The Hit* and Television South's decision to make MacKenzie's *The Aura*.

While the projects initiated by commercial television are by their very nature commercial, the BBC's major film drama productions, none of which have had a theatrical life, have lacked both the cutting edge of commercial popularity and the ambition of art. Films such as Claude Whatham's *The Captain's Doll*, Gavin Millar's *Weather in the Streets* and Michael Lindsay-Hogg's *Doctor Fischer of Geneva* derive their style more from the BBC's traditional concern with costume drama than from the aesthetics of cinema. The boardroom uncertainty as to whom to appoint in succession to the BBC's drama head Keith Williams, who left the post in early 1984, and the confusion within the Corporation as to whether it should adhere to the public service principles on which it was founded, or read the prospect of cable and satellite systems as a mandate to plunge into the heady world of commercial film-making, clearly indicate that it will be some time before creative film-makers can expect any succour from this source.

Film-financing is always a hit-and-miss affair. Interesting scripts are ignored while dross gets financial backing. Film-makers with exciting ideas are pigeon-holed as private film-makers, while the exponents of mediocrity are given the chance to make a hash of brilliant scripts. Executives search for an original film that will have the public queueing around the block to get into the cinema, but repeatedly finance the banal and 'safe'. All these are givens in any film industry. Film-makers have to seize the opportunities created by diverse new sources of finance, to continuously challenge those who hold the purse-strings with radically different projects. They must not fall for the easy production that has money attached but demand the right to make something original.

The development of new sources of finance and the expanded opportunities for the exhibition of feature films have created a new optimism among British film-makers. The next section of this book examines the ways in which the new directors look upon these opportunities. These directors do not constitute a movement as such. Some are more concerned with political and social issues, others with the unveiling of personal and psychological preoccupations. The work of several new directors is inspired by an observational approach to the way human beings operate within different social contexts. Others develop subjects that reflect their interest in formal cinematic concerns and artistic expression. All, however, share in a sense that cinema has a potential as a medium of visual expression which has not been touched by television or previous British films. In the following pages I look at their search for subjects that will touch new responses in audiences, and their attempts to establish working methods which will facilitate the full realization of the film medium's possibilities.

# PART TWO

# CREATION

# 5

# DREAMS

In the past twenty years several factors have pre-empted any serious debate in Britain about the nature of cinema. The lack of interesting feature films has given a clear run to those who argue that 'British cinema is alive and well, and living in television'. Those who expressed an interest exclusively in cinema were accused of pursuing a nostalgic quest for a rapidly disappearing entertainment medium. Television films, it was argued, were produced with the same techniques as any feature. Therefore, any limitations perceived in television's output should be ascribed not to any inherent aspect of the medium, but to a deficiency of imagination and aesthetic ambition on the part of those making television films.

Such an attitude ignores certain important differences between the two media. The feature film-maker can exploit the committed nature of the audience and the opportunities created by a large screen and high-quality sound system to produce films of an intellectual and emotional complexity that work made for the small screen cannot match. The creation of cinema films requires a great leap of imagination, to explore the deeper and darker aspects of the human condition. 'We have got to defend,' says Julien Temple, 'the idea of cinema, that concept of seeing things larger than life together with other people. The kind of cinema that takes people inside a screen is a hypnotic experience.'

Despite occasional experiments with non-naturalistic

81

drama, television tends towards realism in all its work. It is the ideal medium in which to narrate the documentary facts about life. Such an approach, to paraphrase the Spanish director Luis Buñuel's account of Marxism, ignores 50 per cent of the reality. The penetrating work of art must chart the realm of dreams and the subconscious. To hide behind the quest for realism is an inadequate response to life's challenges. Carl Jung said, 'The psychic life is full of problems. When we must deal with problems, we instinctively resist trying the way that leads through obscurity and darkness. We wish only to hear of unequivocal results, and completely forget that these results can only be brought about when we have ventured into and emerged from darkness. But to penetrate the darkness we must summon all the powers of enlightenment that consciousness can offer.' Many of the new British film-makers recognize that the ambition of cinema must be to chart those deeper levels of consciousness. 'I really believe,' says Derek Jarman, 'that the cinema should dream. The films that are constructed out of the imagination and explore interior worlds are the valuable ones.' James Scott expresses a similar view: 'In cinema, you deal with myths really, much more subterranean things. Cinema to me is much closer to poetry; it is dealing on levels of feeling and emotion, whereas television is dealing with information and debate.'

Cinema's potential to dream has rarely been recognized by British film-makers in the past. The film-makers of the Free Cinema adopted the principles of realism because their area of attack was on a film culture predominantly oriented towards escapism. In their desire to explore pressing social and personal issues, the espousal of realism gave their films a moral seriousness that forced them to be accepted and considered, whereas something more complex and profound might have been rejected as indulgent nonsense. Some of these film-makers manifest the deficiencies of the realist mode even within their own work. The use of an elaborate structure of flashbacks and dreamlike sequences on the rugby field in Lindsay Anderson's *This Sporting Life*, shows the realist aesthetic grappling with the problems of a form that would seem to deny the working classes a fantasy life. Inner worlds can be explored even within a documentary context. *Nightcleaners*, a film made in the early 1970s about the attempt to organize a group of cleaners into a trade union, is described by one of its makers, James Scott, as being about dreams: 'Nightcleaners don't have much time for dreaming – they have to work all night – but, in fact, everyone dreams and everyone understands dreams. The purpose of dreams is to touch people at a level where they begin to question the meaning of their lives, and to think that life isn't just something to be lived from day to day.'

The new British film-makers are mostly united in their rejection of the realist ambitions of Free Cinema. They appeal to the tradition of British cinema which did make the imaginative leap into inner states of mind and the darker side of life. Notable members of this canon include Carol Reed, whose films, such as *The Third Man* and *The Fallen Idol*, were shot through with moral ambiguity in their depiction of lies, deceit and irrationality; and Michael Powell, the maker of the sinister and voyeuristic *Peeping Tom*, as well as *Black Narcissus*, *The Red Shoes* and *A Matter of Life and Death*. Some plead for a re-examination of the pictures made by Terence Fisher at Hammer Studios. They explored the irruptions of the supernatural – in the form of werewolves, gorgons, vampires and sundry other fantastic monsters – into a bourgeois and aristocratic world. Robert Hamer's work which includes *Kind Hearts and Coronets, Dead of Night* and *Pink String and Sealing Wax* for Ealing Studios has also been neglected. These films explored the dark conflict between the dreams of the individual and the reality of the outside world in a way uncharacteristic of Ealing. 'There's a great tradition of British film-making,' suggests Julien Temple, 'which people tend to keep quiet about.'

Is there any reason why cinema, rather than television,

should be the inheritor of these traditions? Both media rely upon combinations of image, voice and sound to convey their messages. Audiences can 'read' these movies, and others, on the small screen, as is evident from the popularity of films on television and video. They cannot, however, receive the impact of the film intended by its maker. Andrew Birkin finds that 'no film that was wonderful in the cinema fails to work on television, it just worked much better in the cinema.' Others take a more hardline view. For Lynda Myles, 'movies that I really love look wretched on television.' And Bill Douglas says: 'You realize that some films are impossible to watch on the box. When they do work for you on television, it is probable that they didn't work for the people who saw them in the cinema.'

The argument is complicated by the fact that so many cinema screens today are small and, together with poor sound equipment and an unsalubrious environment, they offer cinema-goers an audiovisual experience little better, if not worse, than that available in their own living rooms. In addition, many contemporary films do not make full use of the medium. At the heart of the debate is a serious attempt to define an aesthetic which relates to film's maximum potential. At present, the conditions for the development of film's expressive powers are only available in cinema theatres. By contrast, as Michael Radford argues, 'there are films which, despite their banal construction and melodramatic way of looking at things and rather awkward acting style, you can get away with on television, which you cannot do when they are blown up on a huge screen. If a film works on a large screen, if its drama works and the structure of it works, if its *mise en scène* works, then it is a movie.'

The starting point for a definition of cinema is the size of screen, and the fact that the cinema audience is placed in a position where what is being represented is larger in scale than an individual human being. There are many stories that are too large in scale for television to handle, and certain approaches to stories which explore emotional and physical scale that are simply domesticated within the context of a television screen. Whereas television thrives upon domestic parlour pieces, a movie like Nicolas Roeg's *Eureka*, a story of murderous desperation, overwhelming passion and enormous evil, is beyond its scope. Roeg himself said, after seeing the film on video: 'It is all right as a reference, but that gangster is supposed to be terrifying.' Jean-Luc Godard has said of television: 'It is not very scary, because it is so small and you have no fear of it. But in the movies, the image is frightening. It is big and you look at it from far away.'

The cinema screen offers the film-maker the opportunity to create complex images. The quality of a film-maker's understanding of the medium is reflected in his capacity to make the action within an image complex and meaningful, and to develop that action through camera movements and angles in such a way as to engage the emotions of the audience. Where the film-maker does not use the full resources of the medium, as in the static camera approach adopted by Peter Greenaway in *The Draughtsman's Contract*, the reason relates to the specifics of a particular film. On the whole there is little place in the cinema for static midshots of two people talking against a picturesque background or the 'flip-flop' reverses during dialogue scenes, both so common in television. Television at its best does use all the resources of film, but it can never have the same impact as work for the cinema. In consequence, little encouragement is offered within television for directors to develop visual sophistication, and an expressive style of camerawork which does more than merely follow action and dialogue. 'It was so powerful,' says Stephen Frears, 'when I first came into television. You could just go into the corner of a room and shoot at the end of a long lens and you knew that you had a sequence.'

The cinema screen also offers the film-maker a higher quality image. For Richard Eyre making his first feature, *The Ploughman's Lunch*, was like 'suddenly being allowed to play with capital letters. I was unprepared for the sheer difference in quality and density, that seems to lend itself to much richer textures.' Terry Bedford points out that cinema films can cope with much greater variations of shade, 'enabling the film-maker to make things dark and moody, and create a lot more drama than television could cope with'.

Even in a cramped mini-theatre the relationship between the audience and what is on the screen is very different from the experience of television viewing. Television executives may dispute the fact but, as a general rule, the television audience watches the screen with less concentration than they would apply to a film showing in a darkened cinema theatre which they have paid to enter. A television film is also seen as part of a continuous flow of programming which, as Mamoun Hassan argues, 'means that whatever pleasurable experience you have of a programme is going to be erased by the next one'. Aware that he could rely on the audience's attention, Marek Kanievska felt that he could develop the action more slowly, and move at a steadier pace when making *Another Country*: 'For a television film you have to captivate the audience in the first three or four minutes to prevent them from turning off. Television is so passive. If you have actually left the home, paid your money and put your bum on a seat, there is more of a sense of occasion, and you have a different relationship to the images. The film-maker has got an audience basically there. They have given him far more of a chance.' For Peter Greenaway, 'it is not just a question of whether you use close-ups or bright colours, it is to do with actual attitudes towards looking, the committed sense of the cinema audience against the totally uncommitted television audience, and the complexity of ideas which you can use with one and not the other.'

A cinema movie is generally looked at more attentively in any case, because of the status which it acquires from extensive promotion and long life. Television films will become less transitory as they are recycled by the new media. Currently, it is only the cinema film that has to campaign for its audience over a period of time. Following a film's initial release, it will play in various cinemas around the country and develop, or lose, its significance as it becomes an object of cultural debate. 'It is in the air,' says Julien Temple, 'and it changes as it passes.' That fact influences the director's consciousness when the movie is in production. 'You are faced,' comments Richard Eyre, 'with the momentarily horrifying prospect that you are making a film that there is absolutely no compulsion on anybody to show or watch. It is much more exciting and hair-raising. With television, you know that it is going to go through the machine and be absorbed.' The feature film-maker must work on the basis that, since the work is going to be subjected to a high level of attention over a protracted period, the second-rate and uninspired will not do.

Making a film for a committed audience, the film-maker can use the full range of visual and aural possibilities available in the medium, exploiting style and form to create a pattern of suggestion and innuendo more subtle and far-reaching than anything conveyed within the contained world view of television. 'Cinema films,' says Colin Young, 'deal with the enigma of the image, whereas television drama deals with the explanation of the image. Film is about gaps and leaving things unsaid.' If television tends towards the prosaic, cinema aspires towards a poetic indeterminacy. It works with narratives that lay down clues leading the audience into the mystery, as opposed to the day-to-day facts of its subjects' lives. It works with symbols that convey the significance of events but which are not necessarily explained within the film. Cinema does not have to be understood, but it must be felt.

Cinema gives the film-maker the opportunity to plunge beyond the facts of existence, to explore aspects of consciousness that television cannot touch upon. Television can get away with diffuse dramatization, but a cinema film must have concentration. 'It is a matter of the centre of gravity,' suggests Bill Forsyth. 'In a film the final balance always rests with one character, whereas if something isn't a film, it can wander around a bit more.' A television writer dramatizing Ian McEwan's short novel *The Cement Garden* might be tempted to 'flesh out' all five characters in the story. Andrew Birkin's planned film is faithful to the book's concern with exploring the lonelinesss and isolation of a boy coming to terms with his own adolescence, and the blossoming out of his imagination. The other characters operate only on the periphery. Birkin intends to use the power of images and music to take the audience into the boy's inner world 'so that you no longer know what is actually taking place and what is going on in his dream', and scenes are shot in a subjective way to 'make the audience aware of the dark things that they haven't even realized about themselves'. Birkin's subjective approach is similar to that of Bill Douglas in his *Trilogy* films where all events are seen from an individual boy's viewpoint. The viewer is never allowed to see beyond the central character's often limited perspective.

In the attempt to explore the whole of reality, the film-maker is often driven to create a context that is, in itself, unreal. In Peter Greenaway's film, *The Draughtsman's Contract*, the context is not really the dastardly goings on in the country houses of Restoration England's foppish aristocracy. The exaggerated wigs worn by the characters are sufficient indicators of that. Instead, Greenaway creates an imaginary world, hinged around various aspects of seventeenth-century England, which enables him to explore certain intellectual concepts. Behind all Greenaway's work is a postmodernist sense that narrative structures of chronological succession and logical cause-and-effect are false to the essentially chaotic and problematic nature of subjective experience, and that the patterns we discern in experience are wholly illusory. Greenaway says of *A Walk Through H*, a study of the transmigration of the soul across ninety-two different maps: 'I find it quite interesting that a man goes to great lengths to create a system which is ultimately bogus, although it is useful because it helps him to comprehend the whole thing.'

Greenaway's films do not attempt to give the viewer an assurance of the reality of the subject matter. The very form draws attention to itself and invites the audience to apply its intelligence to the work. Instead of stirring emotions through a naturalistic depiction of characters and situations, his films give audiences an opportunity to stand back and look at malevolence, evil and danger in the world around them. The effect is to increase, not diminish, the audience's emotional response. 'Great reflective art is not frigid,' Susan Sontag has said. 'It can exalt the spectator, it can present images that appal, it can make him weep. But its emotional power is mediated. The pull towards emotional involvement is counter-balanced by elements in the work that promote distance, disinterestedness, impartiality. Emotional involvement is always, to a greater or lesser degree, postponed.'

Greenaway's films are a complete denial of realism, and the fact that many British film-makers scorn Greenaway's work for its 'lack of profundity' is in itself testimony to the stranglehold that realist attitudes continue to exercise on British cinema aesthetics. 'There was some witty dialogue in it,' says one, 'but I found the actual shooting of it very pretentious, and one didn't remotely care about any of the characters. It was an intellectual exercise.' Greenaway says of realism: 'I dislike the area of experience recollected through art. The area of painting I like least is impressionism which attempts to capture the moment. I much prefer classical landscapes — studied, organized and considered. I would suggest that the pursuit of realism is a chimera.'

In a cinema film that is not pure escapism, the difference between reality and fantasy is not necessarily clear-cut. Neil Jordan, who attributes to an Irish upbringing 'a feeling that your imaginative experience is in some way more important than your real experience, and an impatience with the world as it is, with accepting that the facts that surround people's lives are the whole story', doesn't draw any clean distinction between his ideas for 'fantasy' films and others more clearly related to the 'real' world. *Angel* was a contemporary 'story of good and evil and one particular human being who couldn't really distinguish between the one and the other'. His script for a film on Michael Collins relates to a historical character with an equally acute moral dilemma. Jordan does not see those two films as of a fundamentally different order from *The Company of Wolves*, a film written by Angela Carter and based on her retelling of the Red Riding Hood stories. It is a bizarre tale about an adolescent girl and werewolves, but is also 'quite simply about human dreams and nightmares'. He relates his concept of the 'fantasy' film to the surrealist-influenced work of Jean Cocteau (*Orphée, Beauty and the Beast*), rather than the 'silly comic book stories such as *Star Trek* and other recent American productions, which are great fun, but use the resources without really exploring them'.

The association of fantasy with escapism is misleading. It is a charge that particularly galls Bill Forsyth whose film *Local Hero* was roundly condemned by some critics for perpetuating a series of myths about the Scottish Highlands. Forsyth quotes the response of someone from the Isle of Skye who thanked him, after a screening of the film at St Andrews, for making a film which showed what it was like to live in the Highlands of Scotland: 'It wasn't escapist to him, and it wasn't romantic to him, because he was one of the people portrayed in the plot.'

In their search for subjects that allow for an exploration of the deeper aspects of the human condition, the new British film-makers are rediscovering cinematic genres that, being at one remove from reality, enable them to work with a stylized representation of the world. Stephen Frears has made a thriller, *The Hit*, which he describes as an evocation of 'passion, violence and emotion'. Trevor Preston's script for *Bones* tells of a British businessman who has to cope with the transformations in his personal relationships and the suspicions of the police following his seemingly un-motivated kidnapping and un-ransomed release, by a group of German terrorists. Roger Christian's science fiction thriller

*2084*, shot on locations in Australia, concerns the efforts of a young man and his companion 'droid' (a mechanized being with human emotions) to escape from a mining colony on another planet, after overthrowing the brutal and repressive regime that runs the place.

Julien Temple's first dramatic film, *Absolute Beginners*, is based on a book by Colin McInnes about young people in late 1950s London, but will be cast in the form of a musical. It describes the effects on teenage life of the new prosperity, sexual liberalization, and the emergence of new ethnic groups as elements of English culture, but its form has nothing to do with realism. Temple describes the film as an exploration of 'life, an unstoppable flow of vital and sexual forces, the working of energy itself', and sharply distinguishes his concept of the musical from that of Broadway. It is the only form, he believes, which is capable of simultaneously handling the 'contradictions, the pain and the pleasure, the humour and the horror'.

The concern of many new British directors to exploit cinema's ability to articulate dreams and fantasies present something of a paradox. It involves a rejection of television's preoccupation with social issues and domestic dramas, but its orientation is not escapist. The concerns of the 1960s generation with self-discovery and political radicalism come together in an attempt to rediscover the cinema's power to move the attention of the audience away from immediate realities to see the deeper roots of the problems that they confront in the contemporary world, and to dream of new possibilities. The success of this cinematic endeavour will depend on the level of imagination which the new British film-makers can bring to bear on their subjects.

# 6

# SUBJECTS

In the recent past, British film-makers have been caught between two rocks of misconception. The making of films that derived from fantasy and imagination has been condemned as 'escapism'. On the other hand, stories that emerged from British society and history were regarded as the exclusive preserve of television. British-themed films, it was said, would not 'travel' in the outside world. Yet cinema is not limited to the use of certain stories. What matters is the film-maker's success in developing a narrative to transcend immediate realities and explore human depths.

There is little that is new to be told, but there is still much to be said. 'we have been to every corner of the world,' says James Scott, 'we have taken the camera as far and as near as you can possibly go. We can enter right inside somebody's body. We can get into space. Every image of the world has now been seen, but audiences still want to see more.'

The attitude which film-makers adopt to their immediate world varies according to the nature of their personal concerns. Nicolas Roeg's films, for example, often place characters from different cultural contexts in exotic settings where the director's interests in passion, time, love and identity can be fully explored. For Roeg, a preoccupation with the exploration of 'indigenous' themes would be an absurd limitation: 'I think it is not very healthy to lay so much importance on the Britishness of things. There are subjects that are parochial and English, there are others that are general, but human emotion is a universal thing. "If you prick us do we not bleed, if you tickle us do we not laugh" applies to everyone as far as I know. In Shakespeare we have the most perfect example of internationalism of emotion, of beauty and of greatness.'

Other British film-makers draw their themes more closely from real events, whether contemporary or historical. They are not necessarily restricted to Britain, and their concern is to explore the implications of events, rather than just to tell what has happened. While Roland Joffe's *The Killing Fields*, for example, is based on Cambodian history, its subject is also a general one of what happens to individuals when they are caught up in a clash of ideologies.

It is more difficult for a film-maker to explore universal themes within a real context, as opposed to an imaginary story or a genre subject. Gradually however, the new British film-makers are learning how to treat historical events and the major issues of the day in cinema. As David Puttnam emphasizes: 'It requires immense confidence to actually take a long good look at your belly button, and realize that it has an object of interest as well as a subject of interest, but we're getting there.'

The particular problem confronting the new British film-makers results from the failure of writers and directors in the past twenty years to conceive of elements within British life and the contemporary world in general that could be made interesting to audiences worldwide. The exploration of political issues by television generated a sense that everything there was to be said about society was being expressed in that medium, even though television generally limits its impact by wrapping dramatic themes in standards of good taste and neglecting their universal significance. Television's recent turning away from social and political concerns has liberated this area for film-makers. Some socially relevant television drama is still made, such as Alan Bleasdale's *Boys from the Blackstuff* series, but as Mamoun Hassan observes, 'whereas twenty years ago, if you wanted to make a really

interesting film about Britain, you would make it on television, now you do it for the cinema'.

The way in which television drama has absorbed potential
cinema themes and the pervasiveness of its approach to
subject matter provides a challenge to which the new British
film-makers have to respond. The success of television,
contrasted to the failures of cinema, creates the impression
that the British landscape, and more particularly England, is
more televisual than cinematic. The problem of the dominance of television's modes, and the weaknesses of British
visual culture in general, can be responded to in two ways.
Firstly, it can involve a headlong flight from anything that is
familiar from television's representations. Terry Bedford, in
making *Slayground*, deliberately avoided the 'thatched
cottage, country lane, picturesque village and the mews
house in St John's Wood', as too reminiscent of such television thrillers as *Minder* and *The Sweeney* and the 'kiss of
death' for a movie. Stephen Frears will no longer consider
directing any film set in the north of England: 'You have to
bend over backwards to do anything that has any sort of
originality if you shoot there. I really do admire those people
who find new things to say about England, but who *has*
made a new film in England that has any freshness to it?'

The problem can also be confronted. In seeking for an
answer some find a link between the lack of a British cinema
tradition and the weakness of British painting. Lynda Myles
points out how the American western genre took much of its
inspiration from the great landscape painters of the American West, who have no parallels in Britain. Peter Greenaway, some of whose short films are vignette explorations of
the English landscape, concurs: 'England is basically an
uncinematic nation. With one or two major exceptions such
as Turner and Constable, we have nothing to show in terms
of European art. We are not a nation of painters, we are
probably a nation of illustrators.' Greenaway's *The
Draughtsman's Contract* and, in a different way, Chris
Petit's *Radio On* were self-conscious attempts to develop a

94

cinematic way of understanding the English landscape.

Similarly, problems are thrown up in the attempt to make films in London and other English cities. Bill Forsyth argues that the English metropolis has a lack of clear identity. He speaks of his home town of Glasgow as a 'solid, photogenic, urban location which is as good as San Francisco', and suggests that a lot of people in London don't realize that they are fighting for a sense of identity that other places automatically have on offer: 'You cannot retreat into simple things like the East End or Mayfair, because they are just stereotypical now. British film-makers have been trying to find an identity for the south-east of England for fifty years now and have not succeeded.' But the awareness of the problem also implies a fresh attempt to solve it. That is one of the ambitions of Julien Temple's film, *Absolute Beginners*: 'No one,' says Temple, 'has made a film about London which makes the city "cinematic" in the way that Paris, New York or Los Angeles have been treated. In London the image is still that of Ealing or swinging London, which didn't actually show London as a city, but explored shops and clubs.' 'No one,' adds Chris Petit, 'really looks at London, and there are few films about London which really give a strong sense of place.'

The new confidence with which film-makers have begun to explore British subjects owes something to the success of *Chariots of Fire*. It not only gave a commercial credibility to films based on British stories, but it also provided an example, in opposition to which other film-makers could define their ideas. The criticisms generally relate to the film's use of history as a vehicle for nostalgia. Julien Temple for example, considered that the film pandered to the current British refusal to accept the nature of contemporary life: 'It is a million miles away from the mental state of England at the moment. That kind of sentimental patriotism is a very dangerous area, and exactly what Britain doesn't need. It is kidding yourself, hiding behind things that you would like to be true but aren't. It opens you out to complete flabbiness.'

*Chariots of Fire* is, in fact, a perplexing mix of anti-establishment rhetoric and panegyric to British traditions. Harold Abrahams and Eric Liddell are both men of moral virtue with a fundamental respect for patriotic values. One defies the Cambridge university masters who, from a mixture of anti-Semitism and snobbery, rap him over the knuckles for employing a professional coach. Another refuses to bow to pressure from the British Olympic Committee to compromise his religious convictions by running on a Sunday. The film's director Hugh Hudson responded to the polemic within the film's subject: 'the endeavour of the characters against hypocrisy and intolerance, the total bigotry and double standards of the establishment of the time'. He also saw the connection between the establishment attitudes of the 1920s, and the political and social values of the present. Hudson was not, however, temperamentally or intellectually inclined to analyse and question the nature of those establishment codes. Against the charge that the film is deeply reactionary, he has said: 'We need to have a code of values, or individually and collectively we collapse.'

Another British film that has polarized attitudes is *The Ploughman's Lunch*. Here the charge is that the film's all-pervading nihilism and disdainful approach to its middle-class characters fails to explore the real workings of the attitudes that it depicts. The film portrays a radio journalist lacking in a moral centre. He treats his lower-class parents shabbily. He uses an older woman's affection as a means of access to her daughter. Despite his professional responsibilities to explore and analyse he shows no interest in a group of women encamped around a nuclear base, and is willing to distort the truth about history to secure a publishing contract. Marek Kanievska sees the film's faults as lying in the narrowness of its perspective and lack of any real commitment: 'Although quite articulate politically, it is so insular that the only people it can attract to the cinema are those who share those values anyway.'

*The Ploughman's Lunch* was the first direct response by a

British film-maker to the politics of Thatcherism. The Prime Minister herself appears in the film making her victory speech to the Tory Party Conference, and the Falklands War provides the backdrop to the film's revelations about the moral bankruptcy of Britain's media and academic worlds. As such, the film recognizes that the problems of contemporary Britain, whether explored through mystery, fantasy or sophisticated forms of realism, represent a rich subject area for contemporary British cinema.

David Puttnam, who has described the pursuit of contemporary political issues as 'the direction that any serious film-maker working in this country wants to go', senses that it is the emergence of Margaret Thatcher that has given British film-makers a new confidence in the search for subject matter: 'It is tangible in a way that Harold Wilson's government or Ted Heath's policies were not. You can make a film about the repression of civil liberties, or the Greenham Common women, that will find resonances everywhere.' Marek Kanievska observes: 'The oppression that goes on here is quite extraordinary – the press, the manipulation practised by people like Rupert Murdoch, who has Margaret Thatcher eating out of his hand. We have got three million people unemployed and a society that is so divided in terms of class and values. We have the most dated and outmoded educational system. We brought the blacks over in the 1950s, because it was economically convenient, but their culture frightens us because it is so alien to our values, and we therefore feel that we have to oppress them. We must have the guts to portray the power of what people do to one another.'

Marek Kanievska feels that the problem with many earlier British films which touched upon political and social concerns, was that the cinematic passion became lost in the rhetoric. He contrasts *The Ploughman's Lunch* with the work of such German film-makers as Margarethe von Trotta and Volker Schlöndorff, which, within an analysis of the problems confronting German society, 'make their political viewpoints very accessible, because first and foremost they are fascinating films to watch. One can intellectualize about them and work out the politics of what they are saying, but their audiences are much wider because they are fascinating spectacles.'

Kanievska's first feature, *Another Country*, is based upon a stageplay by Julian Mitchell which recounts the emotional events that turn an English schoolboy into a Communist spy. In making the film Kanievska turned the play's relatively gentle critique of the public school system into a passionate attack on an institution which channels the ambitions of its charges solely towards the exercise of power: 'Hopefully people get the feeling that the games people play when they are at school are insane. When you think that for hundreds of years, the people who have governed this country have come from a public school background, where they are obsessed with the fact that they are going to be part of the hierarchy, and with ruthlessly manipulating themselves into positions of power, it seems absurd. Youth is a time when one should be forming ideas, and one should be vulnerable and open.' The film is set in the 1930s but it explores an institution that is still part of British society and examines its relevance to the present fabric of British life.

Julien Temple also finds German models appropriate to his cinematic ambitions. With his film musical, *Absolute Beginners*, he hopes to show the way in which British society has been transformed in the past twenty-five years, in order to counter the prevalent feeling that nothing has changed. He compares the objective of his film to that of the late work of Rainer Werner Fassbinder (*The Marriage of Maria Braun*, *Lili Marleen* and *Veronika Voss*) which sought, through an exploration of the roots of the German economic miracle, to present an analysis of the contemporary situation. He points out that, unlike their British counterparts, no film-maker born into wartime Germany could pretend that he or she hadn't lived through a period of history. Temple sees the British enthusiasm for video as a manifestation of the desire to escape the implications of history for the present. 'I wish,' he says, 'that people would make films that connected with the central aspects of Englishness. I hope that *Absolute Beginners* can play a part in killing off the myths about the early 1960s that are being artificially kept alive, and challenge people to come up with something better by saying, "Look, they did it twenty-five years ago better than it has ever been done since. What are you doing? Don't sit and look back at all that. Go out and create something equally powerful but different, as equally unpredictable as all that."'

Michael Radford is another of the new British film-makers who feels that history is for valuable exploration of the present. His first feature *Another Time, Another Place* was not a re-enactment of the reality of life in wartime Scotland, but a schematized account of a clash of cultures and values. There is also no specific period setting for his film adaptation of George Orwell's *1984*. The film, like the book, is a political essay which examines the spirit of totalitarianism in the context of a human story: 'It is about what happens to people when all human dignity is stripped away, and how this lack of human dignity doesn't exist in a concentration camp, but is institutionalized so that the standard form of survival is betrayal.'

Radford is sympathetic to Orwell's philosophy of radical humanism, which is based on a distrust of all political ideologies which accept that the end can justify the means. 'Such concepts,' says Radford, 'become ends in themselves rather than existing to serve the needs of humanity.' The irrelevance of dogma to modern life is a regular theme in his work. The documentaries *The Madonna and the Volcano* and *The Last Stronghold of the Pure Gospel* examined communities which maintained strong religious convictions that had not caught up with the realities of the modern world. *Another Time, Another Place* tells of a woman who attempts to break out of the shackles of a dour Scottish life to embrace the attractions of Italian culture. 'I have one particular desire,' says Radford, 'which is to say that life is complex, that there are no givens, that the 1980s in Britain is a time for being aware of contradictions and paradoxes. It is as if the world is so complex that any strong beliefs that we have been taught are not capable of piercing it or controlling it. All the things that we were taught to believe in have crumbled away, and there is a sense that in Britain there is no longer any ideology that can cope, except the rather backward ideology of Margaret Thatcher.'

Although Roland Joffe's film *The Killing Fields* is set in Cambodia, and has only one Englishman in the cast, it shares the same English tradition of radical humanism as Radford's film. As its producer David Puttnam says, 'it reflects a sense of fair play, balance and morality which, whether you agree with it or not, is English.' The film shows the attempts of the American government to hold together the Cambodian regime of Lon Nol, by saturation bombing of the countryside where the Khmer Rouge guerrillas were established. *The Killing Fields* questions values that place ideological victory before human life, and ascribes the responsibility for the barbarities that followed the American defeat to previous American policies in the area.

Joffe contrasts the thematic complexity of *The Killing Fields* to the simple logic of *Casablanca*, a film which explored similar issues but resolved them in a different way: 'What fascinates me about this film is that it is using similar imagery but the solution is no longer getting on airplanes and committing yourself to a cause. Finally all ideologies are initiated by, and transmuted through, people. Therefore no idea is better than the culture whence it comes. History is quite often the unexpected result of unexpected actions of people in unexpected situations. *The Killing Fields* puts human beings first and tries to look at the effect on them of being caught up in historical circumstances, and the clash of ideologies. One of the sadnesses of Cambodia and Vietnam is that two ideological powers have been fighting proxy wars there. What has been fascinating is to look at some of the real complexities and the real human issues involved in that.'

A similar concern with the relative importance of people, rather than ideologies, is reflected in the other film produced by Puttnam in 1983 – *Cal*. Adapted by Bernard MacLaverty from his own novel, the story is set in contemporary Belfast, and presents the dilemmas confronting an Irish Catholic boy who is under intense pressure to join the IRA. He was involved in the killing of a Protestant in front of the man's wife, and it is to her farmhouse that he turns to escape his republican mates. His love for her, and the way in which it is reciprocated, removes any residuum of the ideologically conditioned hatred which he is meant to feel for Protestants as a group. 'A lot of people in the Provos,' says director Pat O'Connor, 'are like that – working class and unemployed. It is very easy to be drawn or pressured into it. Once you are in, it is very difficult to get out.'

It was often asserted in the 1970s that British subjects did not lend themselves to cinematic treatment. The best British film-makers could hope for was to make meaningless films set in nowhere places, under the pretext of exploring universal emotions. The transformation into cinema of any significant subject from recent history or contemporary politics does present major problems. The pull of reality can limit imagination and interpretation. It is a challenge that British film-makers must confront. Previous campaigns for the right to make 'indigenous' movies were fought from a narrow perspective, but it is a fact that many film-makers are stirred by the social and political developments which they see in their own world. If they are not able to make films which pursue those concerns, they will be less likely to find an outlet for their other passions.

# 7

# SMALL FILMS

Jean-Luc Godard's film *Prénom Carmen* carried a dedication: 'In Memoriam Small Pictures'. That expression of regret at the way in which the pressures of commercialization have made the production of innovative low-budget pictures almost impossible reflects a problem faced by all contemorary film-makers. A film necessarily costs a lot of money. The larger the budget, the more licence a director has to develop stylistic sophistication and visual impact, but the less opportunity he has to be spontaneous and take risks. With the decline of regular cinema-going, film financiers prefer to risk their cash on the spectacular and grandiose than on the small and rough. Television has the resources and the audience, but not the motivation, which would provide the basis for producing a range of relatively experimental and cheaply priced movies. The only solution to this conundrum lies in film-makers being able to tap the resources of television to work autonomously in the creation of cinema. In Britain such a link-up between the two media has not been tried, until recently. In Europe the relationship between cinema and television has been more fruitful, but always fraught with tension and conflict.

In Britain the ambitions of film financiers have generally been inflated. Yearning to break into the American market and never content with the more modest returns available from the release of a picture in Europe and sales to television, they have tended to cling to the theory that unless a film is made for a certain price it stands no chance of securing commercial success. 'We were always reacting to what was in America and what we perceived as being the rules which the Americans laid down,' says David Puttnam. High budgets and big names, rather than style and vision, seemed to be the most appropriate way of defining the difference between cinema and television. The opposite view – that an expensive film has to work harder to get its money back, and casting name artists in place of the people most appropriate to a film's subject can only harm the film – has carried little weight.

Another factor in the elevated budget levels for British films has been the control exercised over the production process by the Association of Cinematograph, Television and Allied Technicians and other labour organizations. The agreements made by these unions with the British Film and Television Producers' Association (BFTPA) are designed to protect technicians against exploitation by producers of major American films shooting in Britain, but they have not allowed for real flexibility in crewing and salary arrangements on smaller films. The Association of Independent Producers has regularly held discussions with the ACTT and other unions regarding the possibility of a low-budget feature agreement, which would entail actors taking deferments on their salary against potential revenues and all-in deals for the crew. However, it is only the British Film Institute Production Board which, to date, has managed to dent union-imposed norms. Through its agreement with the ACTT, the BFI was able to bring in *Ascendancy, The Draughtsman's Contract, Golddiggers*, Sally Potter's *The* and Hugh Brody's *1919* on budgets of around £250,000.

At the same time the budget levels imposed on films financed by Channel Four have generated an awareness that through the imposition of firm financial disciplines it is possible to make pictures on budgets much lower than were previously considered normal. The first six of the *First Love* series made by Enigma Television for Goldcrest and Channel

Four all came in at less than £500,000. That figure included shooting on 35mm film (most of the BFI films were made on Super 16mm) and unlike the BFI pictures, making upfront payments to artists to clear the films for overseas sale. Chris Griffin, producer of the six films, emphasizes that a film does not have to look cheap just because it is made on a low budget and lists among the elements required to keep to such a price: restricting the shooting schedule to between three and four weeks; minimizing unnecessary expenditure on period costumes and set decoration; and not paying the sort of salaries available for those working on major US pictures. It also involves intensive preplanning, with the participation of director and crew.

There are some who argue that the restrictions on stylistic freedom imposed by a low budget are bound to make the resulting films uncinematic. As Alan Parker observes: 'Any form of visual choreography is a difficult and laborious thing to achieve – to lay your tracks, to get the camera movement right, to get the zoom right as the dolly is tracking, and to get the actors performing in exactly the right place. If you are just shooting a film in four weeks, however brilliant and imaginative you are, you can still only do certain shots. Automatically that means "talking-head" cinema. I wonder whether it *is* cinema.' Roger Christian remarks that to make *2084* for £3,000,000 he cut out a lot of camera movements that might have been appropriate and rely on static shots which could be strung together in the cutting room. 'Because of the scale of the budget,' Brian Gilbert says of shooting *Sharma and Beyond*, 'you strip away shots and modify your ambitions and creative desires.'

Some compensation for the lack of stylistic freedom is provided by the high level of commitment given by those working on low-budget productions, who are doing it for love more than money. Peter Greenaway says that while making *The Draughtsman's Contract*: 'There was a great rapport resulting from the fact that it was low budget and nobody had been paid enormous sums of money. There were no star dressing rooms, there wasn't the time, opportunity or inclination for any sort of razzmatazz. I think one of the reasons why the film was successful was that people worked long hours, sometimes seventeen in a day, and put a lot of their own ideas into it.' The challenges thrown up by low budget levels sometimes result in creative innovations. When an ambition towards realism is abandoned, the apparent limitations can be exploited to open up new areas of imaginative film-making. Richard Loncraine observes that the 1930s film *Goodbye Mr Chips* may have been shot on terrible, cheap studio sets, but achieved wonderful things with false perspective and foreground miniatures: 'Film has lost its ability to be theatrical. There's a sort of old-fashioned fantasy approach that allowed one to take people into a world that they couldn't see elsewhere.'

Large budgets not only discourage risky innovations, but also enforce an institutionalized way of thinking about what pictures should be about, and how they should be made. Chris Petit describes the effect of these two factors as a kind of cinematic middle age: 'People have got to a kind of position where they believe that there is money around and that films have to cost a certain amount. There is this ladder that, once you are on, you have to go up – £800,000 for one picture, £1,000,000 for the next, and so on. If films were made in a more flexible and less pressurized way, you could make more mistakes and try things that wouldn't necessarily work.' Stephen Frears feels that the pressure on a director to come up with a masterpiece every time works against experimentation: 'Most of the films that I grew up with weren't huge works of art, and what I liked about them tended to be very small things: things that gave you constant levels of enjoyment and fantasy, and set your imagination going.'

The fact that every contemporary film is a one-off has deprived film-makers of any form of production continuity in which to explore their personal vision and develop stylistically. Frears considers that the freedom allowed to the early Hollywood film-makers to make a film that was thematically linked to a previous one rather than 'original', must have been very constructive as a learning process: 'I would love to go and make another film in Spain with the same characters as *The Hit*. I could make a whole new series of decisions, because I wouldn't want to repeat myself. For directors like William Wyler, the whole process was, "I've killed five people this year, what about a new way of killing someone, or a new way of a guy betraying his wife?" So, you were making a series of quite practical decisions.'

Chris Petit speaks of the difficulty of making films with the sense of spontaneity that is inherent in the early films of Godard, which were made 'like letters, with this sense of petals being hurled into the void, things being dashed off with a certain kind of urgency', and regrets that it is difficult to establish a similar working mode for himself: 'You have lay-offs for two years but the only way you can try things out is to actually shoot them.' Peter Greenaway has the impression that Godard's films functioned as 'links in a chain', raising issues and pursuing ideas in a consistent development: 'You have the sense that, even if one film he planned to make was somehow aborted or postponed, he would come back to it. There's a necessary order.'

The pursuit of film subjects that are 'major' and 'significant' has also deprived British film-makers of the opportunity to sharpen their creative teeth on low-budget genre pictures. But it is possible that the expansion of the UK video market, which has an insatiable appetite for anything horrific or fantastic, will create new chances for British directors to work in this area. Roger Christian decided after making the £5,500,000 film *The Sender* for Paramount Pictures, that he would rather 'work as a smaller film-maker' and has financed his science fiction thriller *2084* through World Film Alliance, a joint venture which includes the UK video distribution company VTC. 'The industry,' he says, 'has to change to survive. We are still making large-budget films, but there is a voracious market in video which could be a godsend for film-makers. With video money, you can make extraordinary and visionary films for a reasonable budget with which you can explore your own path as a film-maker.'

Another aspect of the turning away from Hollywood's precepts is the discovery by some directors that people are more important to their films than large vistas, high technology and special effects. Richard Loncraine found that a persistent element in the response of American audiences and critics to his film, *The Missionary*, was that it exploited a 'humour that came out of characters, rather than one-line gags, and had a gentleness that hadn't been seen in British films since the days of the Ealing comedies'. Roger Christian points to the ability that other European film-makers have to create films around very small incidents: 'Claude Chabrol saw a thing in a paper about someone murdering somebody with a kitchen knife, and created *Le Boucher*, a small, tight and very frightening thriller. Similarly, Polanski's *Rosemary's Baby* has just three characters, and no special effects. Still, it was one of the most disturbing and exciting films of all time.' Pat O'Connor also admits to a limited enthusiasm for films of epic scale: 'What involves me are the ways in which people watch each other, the poignancy of particular moments in a film where you get the lighting, the beauty and the form right.' He mentions such films as Federico Fellini's *La Strada*, Ingmar Bergman's *Wild Strawberries* and Jiri Menzel's *Closely Observed Trains*.

Channel Four has opened up the 'small film' area. David Puttnam, who acclaimed the first batch of Channel Four movies as films 'the like of which many of us had lost hope of seeing in our own language, arriving like a gift from the gods in a parched land', has himself been using the new television channel as an outlet for a series of slight but amusing films under the *First Love* banner. Puttnam's instinct that there was an unfulfilled desire among cinema audiences for observational comic films was justified by the enthusiastic response of New York audiences to *Experience Preferred – But Not Essential*, a *First Love* film directed by Peter Duffell which told of the experiences of a teenage girl working as a waitress at a resort hotel. The influential New York critic Vincent Canby headed his review: 'Pst, How About A Good Little Movie', and spoke in glowing terms of the 'small, sweet English comedy', that promised to be around a lot longer than some of the other, far more ambitious, and expensive new films. 'The film found an audience,' suggests Puttnam, 'that has always been sitting there and which we ignored. In a funny way, we ignored it in our arrogance.'

*Sharma and Beyond*, another film in the series, written and directed by Brian Gilbert, tells of the romantic meeting between Stephen, a science fiction fanatic, and Natasha, the spoiled daughter of a noted science fiction writer. Gilbert describes *Sharma* as an 'ironic comedy, a comedy of social manners. What is intended is that the surface should reveal depths. You don't take things at face value. Motives are mixed, and revealed in glancing and indirect ways.' Gilbert feels that the portentousness of many British movies derives from the self-lacerating guilt about their class origins which afflicts many directors, making them uneasy about dealing with middle-class subjects: 'The fear of complacency, the fear of pretension; there are too many negatives restraining British directors and writers.' The sense of middle-class *mauvaise foi* has carried over, in his view, into a heavy and alien aesthetic style, derivative of expressionism and surrealism. Gilbert observes this trait in the films of Michael Powell and the documentaries of the Grierson school, whereas he traces his own stylistic roots to the films of Renoir and the French *nouvelle vague*, which have a 'freshness in the way that things can seem natural and accidental and breathe – accidental framing, a roughness, a naturalness, a certain insignificance in the placing of the human figure'. By contrast, the influences which have predominated for English film-makers have been 'highly inappropriate to the English character which tends towards irony, understatement, indirectness, subtlety, dry humour, satire and a certain comic edge, without going into caricature'.

If Gilbert's film is based on an observation of certain middle-class subjects, Bill Forsyth's films develop a fascination with the ordinary side of people. The dichotomies, for example, in *Local Hero* arise from the contrast between the public lives of a group of oil executives whose activities play a major role in structuring the economies of Scotland and parts of the Third World, and their normal human desires for love, peace of mind and some access to the mysteries of the universe. In *Comfort and Joy*, a successful disc jockey, abandoned by his girl friend, discovers how limited his life is despite the appurtenances of fame and prosperity. 'Ultimately,' says Forsyth, 'I am trying to celebrate everything as ordinary, in a very self-conscious way.' Forsyth shares with Gilbert a dislike of heavy dramatic modes: 'I don't like art and dramatic situations. I just want to penetrate people's lives on the basis that everything ultimately is ordinary. I want to highlight that ordinariness, to penetrate it rather than to dramatize it. To make something special when in fact it isn't seems to me to be a denial of the very thing that the film is trying to create or glamorize. The purpose of humour in my work is to defuse any hint of dramatic artifice that might be creeping in.'

None of the new British film-makers are free from the desire to work within budget levels that give full scope for the exercise of their visual and stylistic talents. The problem is that the concentration of film industry resources on medium and large-budget films brings with it many disadvantages. Since it takes a long time to raise the finances for, and set up, a major film the production process becomes very sluggish, as even Alan Parker acknowledges: 'The problem is that I can only do so many films in a period. I would love to do more work.' The pressures on a film-maker working within an elevated budget also deprive him or her of the opportunity to innovate with new subjects and original ways of shooting films. Had Bill Forsyth, for example, not found a way to explore the cinematic potential of his personal vision in two low-budget films, he could never have had the opportunity to direct the £2 million-budgeted *Local Hero* in his own distinctive style. The vitality of any film production sector is therefore dependent on the willingness of film-makers occasionally to sacrifice large budgets for creative freedom.

# 8

# VISION

The development of a visual style appropriate to a particular film subject depends on three elements. The director must have a broad understanding of cinema language and its potential, derived from an appreciation of other films. He or she must have worked sufficiently in the medium to know how to exploit the full repertoire of effects in composition, lighting, camera movements and sound. Only when these two elements have been absorbed can the director rely on an instinctive response to a subject to articulate a visual mode for the film. The film-maker with an insufficient grasp of technique and history is likely to fall back on experimental explorations of the medium's workings or a style heavily derivative of other films. A director lacking in personal vision will concentrate on stylistic pirouettes rather than the application of technical ability to the expression of meaning. 'Every story,' says Jeremy Thomas, 'dictates its own style. It should be natural to the film-maker, not a matter of thinking about other films. The film takes on a life of its own, and the style evolves from the director. A film director is an artist and should be allowed to work as such.'

Many of the British experimental film-makers of the 1970s compensated for their lack of technical understanding by applying theories developed as means of criticism to the process of film-making. Film language was reduced to its bare essentials and the barren nature of the films was partially obscured by a barrage of political justifications.

'Film,' pleads Peter Greenaway, 'has painfully put together its vocabulary over the past ninety-five years. Why chuck it all out? I can understand the aversion to commercial and industrial modes of pushing out third-rate propaganda for the activities of industrialism and capitalism, but I don't really see why you need to throw away all the language. Let's try to embrace all that has been learned so far, and use the fullest vocabulary to embrace new ideas.'

The creation of a referential cinema, packed with allusions to other films, has more complex roots. It is a natural recourse for the novice film-maker who is conscious of the enormity of the cinematic past and seeks to build a platform for the evolution of a personal style. It is sometimes part of a constructive attempt to revitalize current film language by drawing upon the styles of older film-makers and other contemporary traditions. It can also reflect a lack of confidence in personal vision engendered by the pressures of commercial film-making. Neil Jordan observes, 'Since people don't get a chance nowadays to make mistakes – films cost so much and so many people want to be directors – one of the ways of covering your tracks is to compose with an eye on John Ford.'

The allusive nature of Chris Petit's first two films was partly a reflection of his own origins as a film critic, but also resulted from his sense that British films had found themselves in a cul-de-sac. The problem confronting Petit as he prepared *Radio On* was: 'What do you make a film about in England, and how do you tell English stories in cinema?' He found his answer in the cinematic approach of the German film-maker Wim Wenders, whose style is reflected in the film's abstract treatment of landscape, its use of rock music and the regressive nature of the central character. *An Unsuitable Job for a Woman* was an attempt to make a more accessible film, this time taking as its source the studio-bound films of Sirk and Lang. His third film was originally to have been made as *Flight to Paris*, and would have explored the workings of an informal camera style, derived

112

from Godard and Rivette, on a subject with British elements. That intention was changed when the location switched to Berlin.

Despite their allusions to European and Hollywood traditions Petit's films contain many original and uniquely British elements, and through the first two films Petit developed confidence in his personal style. 'Flight to Berlin,' says Lynda Myles, 'will kill off the impression that Petit is a Wenders clone, because it doesn't look like anyone else's work.' But many of Petit's contemporaries feel that his derivative approach to film-making detracts from the films' impact. 'The germ of the idea is there,' says Kanievska, 'but in terms of bringing the whole thing together and giving it life, it doesn't work.'

In The Draughtsman's Contract, Mrs Talmann suggests to the draughtsman that the 'intelligent man knows too much'. The artist who grasps all the options, Greenaway suggests, loses contact with the inspiration and the spontaneity necessary for creation. Similarly, a film director must forget cinema history and the technical aspects of film-making if he is to create a film that has any freshness. A director making a thriller knows that the genre traditionally calls for dramatic point of view shots, tracking shots and other forms of expressive and subjective camerawork, with associated lighting and shock effects. In a comedy, on the other hand, such a style is totally out of place. The camera tends to stand back and be very objective. Every film, however, is original and calls for a style that is unique to itself.

A central challenge for the film-maker is to find a way of using the camera to express the film's main themes. 'The camera,' says Pat O'Connor, 'is a wonderful device for building up an overall picture of people, through exploring small gestures that you cannot possibly convey in dialogue. If you are careful, you can make every character interesting and get at the truth of things.' Learning how to use the camera is an essential part of any film-maker's training.

'You never move a camera,' suggests Alan Parker, 'when you first put celluloid through it, because you don't know how to. To track on anything other than a straight line is amazingly difficult.'

For Neil Jordan, 'The moving camera is the whole magic really. The camera expresses the relationship between the actor and the background environment. You can start tight. Somebody else can come in and pull you around. Then you can take in and explore the details of a tree, and so on.' Jordan particularly admires the way in which the Soviet film-maker Andrei Tarkovsky (*Mirror, Stalker, Nostalgia*) uses slow tracking shots to continuously modify images. 'The best moves are the most imperceptible. Because you are not aware of the camera, you just feel the emotional impact of what is there.' The camera involves the audience in the action of the picture. 'If the camera,' observes Andrew Birkin, 'is totally static and objective, allowing people to walk in and out of shots, the audience is completely unmanipulated by the film-maker. That is fine to start a film off, but after a while you want to know the way you are meant to be feeling and where the film is going.'

The moving camera is not essential to expressive cinema. Sometimes there are so many other elements in a film working on an emotional level that a moving camera would only be a distraction. It was in reaction against the florid and seemingly unmotivated camera movements in Jean-Jacques Beneix's *Diva* that Chris Petit determined to compose very static images in *Flight to Berlin*: 'I looked at a lot of 1930s Hollywood films and was surprised to see how little the camera moved. It is a false assumption that if you move the camera, the film is more interesting and moves faster.' Peter Greenaway similarly dismisses the criticisms of the static style he employed in *The Draughtsman's Contract*. The audience was meant to look at the action of the film in a relatively objective way: 'The film is about painting, and as paintings don't move, so the camera doesn't move.' The emotional potency of the music, soundtrack, words and visual images meant that camera movements would have overloaded the film.

The camera is the means whereby the film-maker expresses his view of a subject. When Pat O'Connor made *The Ballroom of Romance*, a television film distinguished by its 'cinematic' qualities, he was attempting to capture the spirit of a 1950s dance hall in Ireland. A predominant image was that of people pasted against the walls, reluctant to join in the action: 'I liked the idea of just holding on stillness, not cutting over and back. These people are rooted and have no way out. I was interested in getting at the subjective reality.'

A director can only use the camera meaningfully if he has a coherent vision of the subject. 'The only way,' says Neil Jordan, 'that the images I make will be worthwhile is if they come straight from my instincts as a director. If I am too aware of the way things have been done in the past, that will cripple me. Everything is an area of choice – even a little colour on the ground. The best way to do it is to work on one's instinct for the whole picture.' Although Jordan's first film *Angel* has been compared by critics to a host of B-movie thrillers and particularly *Point Blank*, the first Hollywood film by John Boorman who produced *Angel*, Jordan himself claims a certain innocence of cinema history: 'I quite honestly didn't know what the term *film noir* meant. I had seen quite a few films that the term referred to, but I wasn't acquainted with all the ideas and classifications developed around the history of films.' The imagery in the film – jazz songs, the dance hall, the saxophonist, the hut by the sea, the waves on the beach – do not directly derive from previous genre films, but are recurring items in Jordan's fiction. One attraction of cinema for Jordan is the freedom that he feels from any sense of tradition: 'One of the problems that I found as a writer in Ireland was that the heritage and sense of the past was almost crippling. To deal with fresh, simple and very real things that affect my own country it is a great help to go into an area that, for me, is totally untouched.'

Whatever the subject of a film the director has to find a

way to become involved in the subjective realities of the characters on the screen and to find resonances in the story that will enable him or her to give the film some weight. In Michael Radford's view, 'film-making is a matter of going out on the set when you do not know what you are going to do and being able to improvise, but still retain a style'. He observes that the tradition in Britain has been to diminish the importance of a personal approach to subject matter: '*Not* having a vision seems to be the quality that you need to make pictures. It is the old artisan "let's get down to it and not be pretentious" approach.' 'Too many films,' says Nicolas Roeg, 'have no heart, but just stop at the screen. You never feel touched by the people, or come to understand their problems.'

To emphasize the importance of instinct and vision is not to argue that film-makers should not be conscious of style or ways of making a message comprehensible to an audience. Bill Forsyth, who made several evidently 'experimental' films before directing *That Sinking Feeling* and the popular *Gregory's Girl*, claims to think of himself still as an experimental film-maker: 'The thing that interests me about anything that I do is not the story but the use of film and the way that film manifests itself behind whatever surface there is.'

However, the controlling element in the rendering of a film subject must be the personal vision of the director. To acquire that vision of a subject that is outside a director's own experience requires an immersion in the context of a film. Many directors do extensive research in art galleries and photographic collections before starting to shoot a film. When Marek Kanievska was preparing to shoot *Another Country* he carried out numerous interviews with contemporary public school boys. Through those discussions he discovered the film's central theme; 'that peculiarly English way of pretending that not much is happening despite the political and emotional turmoil that is bubbling beneath the surface'. With the ambition of the film established it is then possible to make the many decisions necessary to give the film a coherent style: 'You break the overall feel down into hundreds of little components. What do I want to tell the audience about a particular scene? If I cannot answer that, I cannot shoot the film. Then, what is the best way of shooting the film to get the maximum out of what the film needs at particular points? What has happened before, what is going to happen next? I begin to feel the film in terms of a pace and an attitude.'

The creation of a significant and visually interesting cinema is dependent upon directors being allowed the resources, time and opportunity to develop a personal approach to any film. A film-maker with a minimal grasp of cinema history and little technical knowledge but a strong personal vision is more likely to make a meaningful film than a technically skilled director with no idea how to give the images power and resonance. But no matter how experienced a director may be, he cannot be expected to make an interesting picture when he has not had the chance to participate in developing a script and evolving personal ideas around its subject. 'What art is about,' says Michael Radford, 'is the quality of thought and how it is expressed. If a film doesn't have that, it does not matter how many camera movements it has got. It has got to have vision, simple vision.'

# 9

# COLLABORATORS

The director plays a central role in the creation of a stylistically coherent and visually interesting film, but the contri-
butions of many other people are essential. The *politique
d'auteur*, as articulated by the directors of the French New
Wave, was an important step towards defining the right and
the responsibility of a director to mould a film within his or
her personal vision, rather than submitting to the immutable
diktat of a written text or a stubborn producer. It would not
be desirable, however, for films to be made in such a way
that the director's contribution was the only one of any real
consequence. The director's vision acquires new aspects
through his or her creative collaboration with the producer,
cinematographer, art director, actors and others. Within this
team, the director can still put his creative stamp on a
particular film. The main concern for the new British directors is to find ways to become more effective by maximizing
the potential of all the collaborators in a film project.

Most of the producers associated with the new directors
do much more than just raise money for projects. To a
greater or less degree they all play a role in steering films
through the development and production processes to their
marketable form. Throughout they both represent the interests of financiers and assist the director, to ensure that the
best film is made within the resources available. David
Puttnam considers that the increase in the number of
creative producers working in Britain is a promising sign for

the future: 'One of the reasons,' he suggests, 'that cinema here has suffered so badly was the lack of producers who could help directors in a collaborative way to get their films made. That involves actually working on the film idea, developing the screenplay and helping with the casting.' While an experienced director may be aggravated by such an extensive level of producer involvement, most of the young British directors recognize the value of the producer's contribution. The situation is very different in France and some other European countries where the producer is generally seen as an oppressive figure.

No British producer is as active as David Puttnam in initiating projects and promoting young directors' careers: 'I don't just want to be a banker to someone else's ideas and execution. I need a sense of ownership, which I can only get from developing my own material and bringing someone in.' It is also Puttnam's personal view that producers are more likely to initiate ambitious film ideas than most directors: 'Where a producer can get his fun involves a degree of imagination and a degree of stretch in concept that might not always appeal to a director.' It was with a newspaper cutting and a screening of *Whisky Galore* that Puttnam briefed Bill Forsyth on the script for his first medium-budget film, *Local Hero*. An article by the *New York Times* journalist Sidney Schanberg was the source for Bruce Robinson's script of *The Killing Fields*, Roland Joffe's first feature film. It was Puttnam who thought of making a film from Bernard MacLaverty's novel, *Cal*. Although to date he has been actively involved in all the aspects of making a film, Puttnam allows directors the scope needed to develop an individual approach to the film.

Other producers work in close partnership with particular directors. Producer Simon Perry and writer-director Michael Radford, having completed the Radford-initiated *Another Time, Another Place*, hit upon the notion of filming George Orwell's *1984*. Christine Oestreicher and James Scott are partners in Flamingo Pictures, which developed *Loser Takes*

*All* as a feature film. Michael Hamlyn produced Julien Temple's pop promos and documentaries, while doing the initial work on *Absolute Beginners*. While producers such as Jeremy Thomas (*Eureka, Merry Christmas, Mr Lawrence, The Hit*) and Clive Parsons (*Britannia Hospital, Party, Party, Comfort and Joy*) take a less active role in developing projects, it is often the encouragement they offer to writers and directors that enables a film to be written, then made.

The *auteur* theory has permeated film criticism and writing about film for the past twenty years. In an article on the prospects for a revival of British cinema, written in the spring of 1983, the critic Chris Auty suggested that a 'new aggressive breed of intellectually motivated writer-directors' was required to 'drag the existing British cinema in new directions and away from old dramas'. While it is true that those directors who see their role merely as the artisan-like interpreters of scripts are unlikely to develop new notions of cinema, there are permutations in the relationship between writer, director and producer which do allow for the creation of a new cinema aesthetic.

Britain is currently well endowed with writer-directors such as Bill Forsyth, Peter Greenaway, Andrew Birkin, Bill Douglas, Neil Jordan, Chris Petit and Brian Gilbert. There are other interesting directors including Roland Joffe, Richard Eyre and Michael Radford, who are primarily visualizers of other people's concepts, but have written their own scripts from novels and play an active role in developing scripts primarily written by others. Also the writer-directors do recognize the benefits of collaboration. Bill Forsyth developed *Local Hero* within a concept suggested by David Puttnam. Chris Petit brought in a writer to help with the dialogue for *Flight to Berlin*. Neil Jordan, who started directing out of a sense of frustration at the way directors mangled his scripts, found the opportunity to work with another novelist, Angela Carter, on the script for *The Company of Wolves* a stimulating experience: 'Angela's stories are full of the most extraordinary kinds of images, and when we both worked together, we were plucking them out like cherries and stretching them into the narrative form that we devised for the film as a whole. When you work with somebody who is quite different from you, but with whom you share a certain perception, each person stimulates the other into areas that they normally wouldn't explore.'

The notion of the complete *auteur* is a sterile one, in that it denies the specialist skills that a writer can bring to a film work. Its application often results in empty, visual films, deficient both in narrative structure and characterization. The film script provides a structure on which a director can develop a coherent visual style and message. If British films have often been excessively literary in the past, the fault lies with the directors who have failed to develop the visual and dramatic potential offered by the written word. As Brian Gilbert observes, 'English literature has a finesse about it which British directors could well emulate. We have got to face our literature which at its best has all the qualities of film at its best, and more — irony, understatement, indirectness and subtlety.' Ian McEwan, the writer of *The Ploughman's Lunch*, argues that the vapid quality of many contemporary films results from the underestimation of the screenwriter: 'If we are to have a strong independent cinema, which is not looking over its shoulder at French critics and theorists who wish to elevate old Jerry Lewis movies to the status of high art, or at American producers with their ingrained contempt for their audiences, then it would be as well for British cinema to develop its own distinctive qualities, drawing where necessary on our strong literary and theatrical traditions, and transforming them in the process to meet the requirements of film-making.'

The director who writes his or her own script has the advantage of being able to conceive a structure which is inherently appropriate for realization as cinema. Some writer-directors see the preparation of the script as the most creative part of making a film, in so far as it is the time when the visual possibilities of the film are created. As Bill Forsyth testifies: 'I feel more like a film-maker when I am writing because there are no restrictions on how you imagine something happening. There is much less time to be actually creative when you are filming, and in a sense the production process is a series of disappointments.' Bill Douglas has a similar description: 'The film is alive with you when you put your fingers on the typewriter. The film is being made as you write it.'

A script, however, is only a shorthand representation of a planned film – a leaping off point for the director. As Peter Greenaway describes it: 'They are for me a useful balance between content, form and metaphor. In some senses they represent the film, but to quote Godard, "the script is essentially made for the financiers". It has nothing to do with film-making, but is merely a convenient way of showing a producer how the money is to be spent.' The prevalent attitude within television drama departments gives the writer an exaggerated status and allows the director little opportunity to be involved in script development. This approach seriously devalues the role of a director. It is also to be found outside television. 'What happens,' says Michael Radford, 'is that the director is the pinnacle, the conductor of the orchestra, and everyone wants to be him. The result is that everyone thinks that they can. As well as being the most sought-after position, it is also considered to be the one least demanding of competence. Consequently, any writer who has a half-way decent script automatically sees himself directing it. That is why so many British directors are not concerned with imposing a particular vision, but only with turning out a well constructed piece.'

If the writer and director are to establish a constructive and fruitful relationship they must both understand the problems faced by the other, and the contribution that each can make to the film. At the National Film School writers and directors are encouraged to try their hand at both crafts. 'The point,' says Colin Young, 'of writers directing their own scripts is to give them a chance to find out what wasn't in the script. Directors, on the other hand, need to be trained in dramaturgy, so that they understand the construction, exposition and development. They then have some way of interacting with the writer in the process of preparing the film script for production.' Roger Christian cooperated with Matthew Jacobs on the script for *2084* because he felt that 'writing is of the essence of film-making, and the directors who write have a much better understanding of characters and films'.

With mutual understanding it is possible for a director and writer to hammer out a script that is acceptable to the more literary appreciation of the one, and the visual sense of the other. The screenwriter must acknowledge the director's right to call for amendments relating to his or her visual conception of the film, or some aspect of the production requirements: 'Although the script is written and developed,' says Roland Joffe, 'the director knows that the actors have to make it breathe. The writer would be doing it an immense disservice if he said that you must stick to the script as if it was Shakespeare. It just isn't like that.' Andrew Birkin agrees that it is wrong to regard anything as cast concrete: 'There are certain things that I will fight for, usually where I think that the director hasn't understood the intention, but I will readily give in on other aspects.' Equally, the director must acknowledge the values of the script and be prepared to engage in constructive debate. As Richard Eyre describes his relationship with Ian McEwan in developing *The Ploughman's Lunch*: 'We spent hours hammering out what we wanted to achieve, and just marrying our objectives. Sometimes things were changed quite radically, sometimes things remained absolutely unchanged. There was never conflict. I don't think the writer should be treated as a kind of surrogate to the director, or vice versa.'

A combination of flexibility and firmness is required of a director when shooting the film. If he or she arrives for a day's filming without a clear notion of what has to be achieved the production will grind to a halt. The time available for making any film is so short in relation to what has to be achieved, and the number of people with tasks to perform so large, that any form of 'free' improvisation is impossible. 'There was a time,' suggests David Puttnam, 'when films were made by a confused but brilliant guy standing beside the camera with forty-two other people, but not since the days of Max Sennett and D. W. Griffiths.' Marek Kanievska observes that, 'There is no way in which the director can talk to the crew unless he has a very strong impression in his head of the sort of film he wants to make.' Within that overall concept, the director must allow cast and crew to respond with relative spontaneity to the process of production. According to Terry Bedford 'The director's job is to select the good ideas from the bad ones, and generally keep everybody close to the thread of the story. The process is always in flux. You have to be ready to make use of anything which happens that is good. If everything is too rigid, then you have failed to notice the good things that are happening.'

In dealing with actors the director must convey enough of his vision to enable the individual performer to interpret and develop a particular role. A good performance can only emerge from the actor's instinctive response to the demands of a part. Neil Jordan considers that excessive rehearsal can limit an actor's sensitivity to character nuances: 'I find it less important to rehearse than to find out how someone can enrich the part. Rehearsal for me is a matter of sitting down and talking through the role, then hearing what suggestions the actors have and maybe changing a line or more to suit the way they want to play it. I must also know what way they will act, so that I can exploit the performance on the set.' Roland Joffe also attempts to stimulate, rather than direct, performances: 'It is the prerogative of young directors to walk on people's heads with hobnailed boots. As you become more skilled, you realize that you need to do less of that. What you must do is to fertilize people's minds so that their imaginations are working. I put people on overload with information, then say, "just take this at random, don't organize it. That will happen on the day. You have got to be an emotional stuntman and learn how to take risks. You have to trust me to make sure that you land without breaking your ankles." I want to be surprised by the way things turn out.'

Joffe has a similar approach to his dealings with the cinematographer and camera operator. He always hopes that they will contribute more than is asked for: 'It is always slightly depressing when they give me precisely what I wanted. It is a lot better than not getting what you wanted, but the finest cameramen will give you a lot more. One's job is to encourage initiatives and make sure that those initiatives are going in the right direction.' The relationship between director and cameraman is crucial. It is only if the cinematographer understands the director's creative ambition for a film, that he or she will be able to give the picture that 'look' or 'feel' which is appropriate to the vision of the film. As the cameraman will generally have more experience than a director of the technical problems of film-making and the aesthetic consequences of particular ways of shooting, he or she will have ideas about how a particular shot or sequence should be realized. 'If,' says Marek Kanievska, 'the cameraman's approach shows you something you haven't thought of that will reinforce what you feel about a scene, you go for it.'

The calibre of many British cameramen and the breadth of their shooting experience shows in the visual quality of most new British films. Stephen Frears who engaged Mike Molloy, a cameraman with considerable experience on commercials, to shoot *The Hit*, observes: 'Most reasonably budgeted films are being shot to a fantastically high standard by people who shoot fifty weeks a year. They bring so much knowledge and experience.' He adds that their desire to do something fresh and original presents the director with a considerable stylistic challenge: 'You cannot get away with the sort of old-fashioned humanist directing that they were doing ten years

125

ago. You have to match up to their experience.' A number of experienced cameramen, who otherwise work on commercials and high-budget Hollywood pictures, have been willing to work on smaller British pictures. A new generation of cameramen has emerged with an interest in the development of British cinema. The National Film School has produced such skilled cinematographers as Roger Deakins (*Another Time, Another Place*), Syd MacCartney (*Party, Party*), Oliver Stapleton and Richard Greatrex, who often have as deep an understanding of film as the school's director students. Other cameramen, such as Curtis Clark (*The Draughtsman's Contract, Nelly's Version*), Clive Tickner (*Ascendancy, The Ploughman's Lunch, Loose Connections*) and Ivan Strasburg (*1919*) have emerged from documentaries with a similar highly motivated approach.

The process of film-making involves finding solutions to numerous technical and creative problems arising from the director's creative ambition. The film crew is a team which, like any other, functions better after a period of collaboration. 'The most constructive way of making films,' David Puttnam observes, 'lies in a continuous group relationship between people. Film is a group activity, which works when you have a terrific ensemble cast, including good cameramen, sound men and others.' Many directors who graduate from commercials take the key members of their creative staff with them into features. Julien Temple considers pop promos a good opportunity for building up a team of people with a shared working method and approach to film ideas. He observes that 'cameramen who understand your approach to something save a lot of time, but also come up with ideas that complement what you are trying to do'.

A studio system was in some ways the most efficient way of enabling people to collaborate and exchange ideas over a long period. As Al Clark observes of the old Hollywood working method, 'its principal asset was that it gave people a chance to work with each other on a regular basis. The whole debilitating getting-to-know-you process was already obviated. A lot can happen when a large and continually floating number of people just wander in and out of people's lives, exchanging ideas and applying them.' The irregular nature of film production in Britain over the past twenty years has prevented the emergence of stable teams of production. Directors frequently use the same key technicians on all their films, but no director has worked regularly enough in recent years to allow any *ad hoc* feature crews to consolidate and develop distinctive working methods. It is to be hoped that, as production increases in the UK, ways will be found to extend the possibilities for collaborative film-making.

# 10

# CHANGES

The rise in the hopes and competence of British film-makers chronicled in this book is taking place against the backdrop of a transformation in the structure of the audiovisual media through the world. Video-recorders offer audiences new ways of seeing movies. Cable television has already begun to generate new forms, and will have an expanding influence in the 1980s. Audience tastes and responses are increasingly influenced by a flow of commercials and pop promos, as well as the availability of computer games and word processors. This expansion of the media has already generated new funds for production. It also presents contemporary film-makers with a fresh challenge. To create work of any relevance, they must respond to the effect on audiences of developments in audiovisual entertainment.

Some of the new British film-makers take a gloomy view of future prospects. Chris Petit, for example, suspects that film directors will soon be seen as dinosaurs, playing to a concept of cinema that is on its last legs: 'The whole idea of the ninety minute film will change because the next generation has been brought up to think of television images in a completely different way. Everything is more or less the length of a single record. I wonder whether the whole thing isn't becoming more concentrated, and just based on staccato releases of energy.'

Others embrace the new forms as stimuli to the creation of new cinematic styles. The pop promo, the first form to

128

evolve from cable, relies for its impact primarily on images. Julien Temple considers that promos are educating young audiences to a new understanding of images, and opening up new ways for film-makers to tell stories: 'One of the things that I was most surprised to discover was that, with video, you can tell quite a complicated story in four minutes. That kind of intense compression of things is going to be very exciting on the large screen. Also, the film-maker has more freedom to break conventions, because the audience is visually literate.' Peter Greenaway expresses a wholehearted zeal at the prospect of a transformation in cinema: 'Film is only a ninety-five-year-old aberration of visual expression, and already the evidence exists that the cinema is being taken over by new forms. I would like the films I make to be part of the general process of visual expression. Perhaps, if I was making films in twenty or thirty years time, again they would be completely different in format – a post-television form of some description.'

The concern of the new British film-makers is not to descend to the trivial level of the promo, and most other output likely to be generated by the new media. It is to take from the new forms those elements which will enlarge the visual resources of cinema, and to exploit the possibilities created by the new distribution outlets. Video and the repeat-reliant schedules of the cable and satellite television networks will not only expose audiences to more images but also facilitate repeated viewings of interesting films. The best feature films have always contained multiple layers of meaning that are only revealed if the film is seen more than once, but the increased opportunity for repeat viewings of films is a further encouragement for the film-maker to make images, and the relationship between sound and vision, more complex. Films will need to concentrate less on the values of transient entertainment than on the potency of the medium.

The experience of cinema has to date only been available in theatres. When it becomes possible to recreate many aspects of cinema in the home, the range of subjects and styles that can be explored cinematically will be considerably broadened. The technology already exists to create high-definition television images with a picture quality many times superior to the current television picture. Such images can be projected to a scale that will destroy the concept of television as a box that sits in a corner without really challenging the viewer. 'By the year 2000,' predicts David Puttnam, 'we will get to the size, scale and sound quality of cinema circa 1960. Basically, once you reach that point, the experiential quality will be the same as cinema.' The opportunity to offer the cinematic experience in the home will remove many of the problems currently involved in reaching audiences and open up new publics to which film-makers can target their work.

New production technologies will also play a part in changing cinema. Most of the attempts made so far to use the expressive resources of video technology for creative film production have been relatively unsuccessful. Michelangelo Antonioni's *The Oberwald Mystery*, Francis Coppola's *One from the Heart*, and *The Bad Sister* made by Laura Mulvey and Peter Wollen, were leaden works that lost their way in a fascination with technology. Part of the current crisis in European cinema is due to film-makers' perception that the rules are being changed, but new ideas about cinema are not emerging. 'The new technologies,' says James Scott, 'have not yet produced a new way of thinking in the way that lightweight cameras and sound equipment did in the early 1960s. Video should do the same thing because it allows you to shoot at no expense for hours and hours, but somehow it just makes people lazy.' It is, however, inconceivable that in time new creative uses will not be found for the resources of video special effects, and other potentials of electronic image-making.

The challenge for the new British film-makers is partly to discover the cinematic aesthetic which other cultures have been exploring for many years. It is also to create a cinema that exploits all the new visual possibilities. The concurrent developments in culture and technology encourage the hope that from what is now just a chrysalis might emerge a period of interesting British cinema. The past failures of film in Britain present one challenge for film-makers. That the effort to develop an indigenous cinema is also linked to the discovery of something fundamentally new should give a sense of freshness to the endeavour.

The achievements of the new British cinema are, as yet, limited. Some interesting films have emerged. There are many articulate and highly motivated directors, but there has not yet been the opportunity for the new film-makers to show that they can find the themes and the creative resilience necessary to create a major body of work. It is not rash to argue that this group of film-makers is in the process of developing a British film culture of significance. They all bring to their work an understanding not only of cinema but also of the other visual arts. They have a passionate desire to stretch the resources of the medium. The diversity of their approaches to film has already created a new vibrancy in the production sector.

The efforts of the new British film-makers have been encouraged by a gradually evolving production infrastructure. The expansion of the audiovisual media has ended the stalemate situation where television, having almost killed off the cinema audience, made no financial contribution to movie production. The companies which control exhibition and distribution, as well as other organizations involved in supplying the public's entertainment needs, have all recognized the existence of a new demand for feature films. Even the government, so long unsympathetic to the plight of film-makers, has recognized that its plan for the development of a wired Britain will require a flow of films for its fulfilment.

Producers who have emerged from among the directors' contemporaries are keen to provide them with the opportunities necessary to develop their personal visions. At the same time there are cameramen, actors, art directors and others, whose understanding of cinema complements that of the directors, and who want to be involved in the adventure of creating a vibrant new British cinema. 'Increasingly,' says David Puttnam, 'I find that I am talking to technicians who really love movies.'

Cinema has never before been fully part of British consciousness. People used to flock to the movies, but the ease with which the viewing public and British film-making talent was almost completely absorbed by television in the mid-1960s suggests that cinema's potential as a challenging visual medium had been little understood. British cinema has remained rooted in theatrical and literary traditions, standing back from the debates about aesthetics and visual meaning which were taking place on the European continent. Audiences have opted for the inexpensive medium of television, apart from the occasional trip to see *Star Wars* or *An Officer and a Gentleman*, rather than regular exposure to the full impact of cinema – a force mysterious, moving and demanding.

Parallel to the film-makers' discovery of the potency of cinema, there are signs that audiences are turning away from the limitations of television. Despite the arrival of a new television channel, viewing figures for television have shown a decline. The British public has enthusiastically seized the opportunity to see movies on video, and has turned out for the occasional interesting British movie. The excitement felt at the prospect of a British film renaissance in itself suggests a new awareness of a medium that can explore the deeper questions of life, and imagine a way out of current political, social and personal dilemmas.

The new technologies offer British film-makers new means to reach a broad public; new resources to finance their creative efforts; and new forms of expression with which to articulate their message. Barring government ineptitude in evolving policies on cable, satellite and the film industry, British film-makers should be able to confront the challenges and realize the possibilities created by these developments. Most important is the way in which they

132

have already found a new confidence for the forging of a British cinema. 'The trouble with British film-makers in the past,' suggests Bill Douglas, 'is that they have lacked the necessary imagination. It seems that some of the new film-makers have finally learnt to dream.'

# INDEX

134